JUST ONE TASTE...

Wendy Etherington

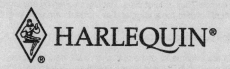

HARLEQUIN®

TORONTO • NEW YORK • LONDON
AMSTERDAM • PARIS • SYDNEY • HAMBURG
STOCKHOLM • ATHENS • TOKYO • MILAN • MADRID
PRAGUE • WARSAW • BUDAPEST • AUCKLAND

ISBN-13: 978-0-373-79267-2
ISBN-10:   0-373-79267-0

JUST ONE TASTE...

This edition published by arrangement with Harlequin Books S.A.

® and TM are trademarks of the publisher. Trademarks indicated with ® are registered in the United States Patent and Trademark Office, the Canadian Trade Marks Office and in other countries.

www.eHarlequin.com

Printed in U.S.A.

"This is nuts. I don't even know your name."

Vanessa put down her wineglass and turned to the man who'd captured her attention. He might be nameless at the moment, but she'd recognize that rebel in sheep's clothing anywhere.

"Lucas," he replied.

"Is that first or last?"

"First. That's enough for now, isn't it?"

For a second she was shocked by the *first names only* suggestion. But it also appealed to her—her daring, defy-all-the-rules side.

First, it was naughty.

Second, if he knew her last name, he'd connect her to her family. And that would end the sparks.

Vanessa's mother would freak if she found out her daughter had picked up a stranger at her fund-raiser. Really, discretion was in order.

And yet Vanessa itched—in more places than her brain—to take a chance. To walk down an unexpected road to see where it led. She was literally on the edge of jumping into this gorgeous guy with both feet.

So she did.

Dear Reader,

Since this is my first Harlequin Blaze novel, I feel the need to confess something important—I love to cook. (All those who hate it have permission to now groan.) In fact, if I wasn't a writer, I'm pretty sure I'd be a chef. But there's no way I'm going to culinary school and working those long, backbreaking hours. Instead, I tortured, er, *created* a heroine who's a caterer.

As you can imagine, I had a grand time with the research for this book. I made tons of my favorite indulgence—double chocolate cheesecake. (I even made those chocolate leaves and curls you see in the cookbook pictures. You can all groan again.) All that dark, rich chocolate made me think of another thing that's better when it's dark and rich…men! Thus Lucas was born.

I hope you enjoy what with luck will be the first of many Harlequin Blaze novels for me. Check out my Web site at www.wendyetherington.com, or I'd love to hear from you at P.O. Box 3016, Irmo, SC 29063.

Best wishes,

Wendy Etherington

ABOUT THE AUTHOR

Wendy Etherington was born and raised in the deep South—and she has the fried chicken recipes to prove it. Though a voracious reader since childhood, she spent much of her professional life in business and computer pursuits. Finally giving in to those creative impulses, she began writing romances. In the past six years she's published eleven books, while still managing to indulge her weakness for making—and eating—double chocolate cheesecake on a regular basis.

Books by Wendy Etherington

HARLEQUIN TEMPTATION

HARLEQUIN FLIPSIDE

HARLEQUIN DUETS

To David Etherington and Jeff Dunn
for their love, support and never-ending hospitality.

1

FROM BEHIND HER POST at the chocolate fountain, Vanessa Douglas watched the posh crowd of Atlanta's social elite schmooze each other.

Prominent doctors and lawyers, board members and business moguls turned out in jewels and designer clothes, decorated by elegantly dressed first spouses or young, hard-bodied second ones. Vanessa fought the urge to yawn.

But when a girl made penis-shaped cakes for a living, a lot of things seemed staid by comparison.

"Have you seen *any* cute guys?" her best friend and business partner Mia Medini asked.

"Nope. And hardly anybody under forty."

"What we expected. Your mother never listens." She planted her hands on her trim hips, which were shown off to perfection in a silky turquoise dress that also complemented her olive-toned skin and dark hair. "People our age go to *night*clubs for fun, not the *country* club."

"Except my sister." Angelica, wearing a powder-blue suit and pearls, stood across the room with a group of elderly women. Nearby, their parents socialized in an intimate circle of longtime friends, her mother in cream-colored Chanel, her father in dignified navy Brooks Brothers. Vanessa glanced down at her rebel-red shimmery cocktail dress, bought from a sample sale in midtown at Vampy Divas. Yep. All was right with the world.

Even though her mother had sent catering business Vanessa's way instead of steering it in the other direction, hell, apparently, hadn't actually frozen over.

"But your sister is a fifty-year-old in a twenty-five-year-old body," Mia said.

"She hooked the best cardiac surgeon in the South."

Mia elbowed her. "Like he's a damn herring. And, personally, he's too staid for me."

"Wearing a bow tie is *not* a good sign."

"Though I once knew this stripper who wore his bow tie on his—"

"Mia, please," Vanessa said, glancing around furtively to see if they'd been overheard. "Not here."

Mia looked wounded. "You turn into such a stuffbucket around them."

She knew it was true. But she was tired of the estrangement from her family. She'd had her rebellion, and she was ready for compromise. "I'm just trying for peace. For once."

"I wish you luck on your journey, Don Quixote."

Ignoring her roommate's negativity, Vanessa rearranged the stack of napkins on the table, which were highlighted by elegant shrimp canapés and delicate chocolate puff pastries. No anatomically correct—or incorrect—body parts in sight.

Damn it.

"Though everybody *has* been complimentary," Mia went on. "You think we'll actually get more business from doing this shindig?"

Vanessa shrugged as if she hadn't given the idea much thought. "Maybe. We could use it."

Of course she'd given the idea *a lot* of thought. Her family was a cornerstone of the swanky society laid out before them. Her father was a senior partner in one of the oldest, most prestigious law firms in the city. Her mother was a premier society queen. Vanessa and her sister had been raised as pristine, pure debutantes.

And she'd chucked it all to slave in the kitchen making chocolate sauce and leaven bread for a living.

Crazy? Her mother thought so. As well as most of the people she'd grown up with. But Vanessa had never felt more normal, free and alive than the day she'd packed her jeans, T-shirts—and the scandalous red bra she'd worn under a white shirt once and nearly sent her mother into a dead faint—and moved out on her own.

After being cut off from the family money at the urging of her mother—she was the power behind the throne, no matter what her father claimed—Vanessa had put herself through culinary school and started her own business. After years of having to *sneak* into the kitchen to help their housekeeper make cookies—debs didn't cook, they nibbled elegantly—she'd found a profession where getting messy was just part of the process.

For years, she'd wondered if the sneaking part was her only attraction to cooking, but after moving out and working in a restaurant, she'd realized that being a chef appealed to her need for excitement and variety. From a practical aspect, she could eat and get paid. Emotionally, it gave her instant gratification—she fed people, and they were happy. She didn't disappoint them, and they didn't try to change her.

Rejection of her efforts was rare.

Which brought her thoughts back to her family. Her sister, believing that a woman wasn't complete until she married, constantly tried to fix her up with men who were completely wrong for her. While Vanessa fought to keep her fledgling catering business afloat, her mother discouraged everyone she knew from using her services. And her father seemed too busy to notice there was a rift in the family at all.

Still, seven years after her big rebellion, Vanessa could say she didn't regret the choices she'd made. She had great friends who supported her, she threw her energy and hopes into her business, and she planned for the future.

And yet…she wanted nothing quite as much as a reconciliation with her family. Just not at the expense of her pride.

How's that for a contradiction?

"Do you think her usual caterer really canceled on her at the last minute?" Mia asked, her tone as suspicious as Vanessa's had been when her mother had called her less than a week ago to ask them to cater this party.

"It's possible."

She'd like to think her mother was softening, or at least getting used to the idea of a daughter in the—*shudder*—service industry. Or maybe, actually—*big gasp*—accepting Vanessa's chosen career and lifestyle rather than doing everything possible to turn her into a society princess and carbon copy of both her and Vanessa's younger sister. But Vanessa wasn't holding her breath.

"I guess I'm a sap for bailing her out," Vanessa continued.

"Since she's done so much to help us."

"She thinks she's doing what's best for me."

"Yeah, well, you're twenty-seven. I'm pretty sure you've figured out what's best for you on your own."

"Hear, hear."

"And we did a classy job. I bet fifty bucks your mother didn't sleep a wink last night, wondering if we'd show up with boob-shaped suckers and a cock-shaped champagne fountain."

Vanessa's eyes widened, and she temporarily shoved aside her vow for peace. She exchanged a knowing look with Mia. "That's not a bad idea."

"For that bachelorette party this weekend."

"We could have champagne spurting out the top."

"Crude, but fun."

"My mother really would faint."

Mia flicked her hand in dismissal. "Well, she's not going to be there, is she? And let's quit talking about her. It's too frustrating." She craned her neck to try to see around and over the crowd. "This place is a crush. Somehow the staid and boring really have found their own place in the world. Imagine that. Still, there's got to be at least one scrumptious, eligible man—*oh, my God.* What's *he* doing here? Hide me."

Vanessa looked around and quickly spotted the problem—Colin Leavy was heading their way. He'd been in love with Mia ever since he'd come into their bakery and catering shop to order a cake for his mother's birthday two years ago. Unfortunately, he was an accountant and the epitome of *staid,* so Mia wouldn't have anything to do with him.

Vanessa thought he was cute, and his devotion to Mia adorable. She might even reveal her chocolate-cheese-cake recipe to have a man look at her with the devotion Colin showed Mia.

Somehow, in her relationships, Vanessa always managed to be the pursuer, not the pursuee. Because she knew what she wanted? Because she knew how to get what she wanted? Or because she impulsively jumped in with both feet without bothering to ask too many questions?

She highly suspected it was the latter, especially after the last guy she'd gone out with that turned out to have a fiancée.

"Good grief," she said to her partner. "There are worse things in life than having a bright, successful man grovel at your feet."

"Depends on the man."

As Colin approached, and Mia realized she didn't have anywhere to hide, she simply crossed her arms over her chest.

"Hi, Mia. Would you like to dance?"

"I'm work—"

Vanessa pushed her friend forward. "She'd love to."

Mia glared at her over her shoulder. "But, I—"

"Come on, Mia," Colin said. "Please."

Who could resist those sweet, puppy-dog-brown eyes?

Apparently not even Mia, who sighed, but held out her hand to take Colin's. Vanessa hoped she let him lead.

While her partner was dancing, Vanessa roamed the perimeter of the room, making sure the platters of appetizers and pastries were filled, and the waitstaff kept the drinks flowing. The party doubled as a fund-raiser for a local children's hospital, so once her mother presented the check to the chairperson at 10:00 p.m., the crowd would probably disperse and Vanessa and Mia would be free to clean up and go. Still, it would be midnight before they got home, as they had to pack everything, then run it all through the industrial-quality dishwasher at the shop.

Dessert First had started on a whim, had quickly become a challenge, but it fulfilled Vanessa as nothing else ever had before.

She'd met Mia in culinary school, where her friend had excelled at organizing and managing much more than she had at cookies and pastries. They'd become close buds, then business partners and roommates. Vanessa knew she could count on Mia like no one else in the world, and that safety net allowed her to handle the tension between her and her family with much more confidence and panache.

Maybe, with Mia's business savvy and Vanessa's sugary concoctions, they wouldn't have to struggle so much someday. Maybe this party could be the beginning of healing and understanding with her family.

Oh, yeah, and maybe the man of her dreams was going to pop out from behind the fruit bowl and whisk her to his castle in the sky.

EXCEPT FOR HER, THE PARTY was a dead bore.

Lucas Broussard prowled the edges of the room, knowing he'd have to endure many more of these things if he was going to be accepted in this city. Networking in his profession was a necessity. A sacrifice, like so many others, he'd just have to buckle down and endure.

Were they all genetically programmed for this stuff? Small talk, gossip, bragging. Trophy wives and pedigreed family trees.

At least, though his mistakes and faux pas were many, he'd never been accused of boring his audience to death.

As expected, and like everyone else, he'd flashed his Rolex. He wore a custom-made designer suit. He'd made plenty of money as a respected attorney, even if the money was a little too new to be decent and his tactics were sneered at by some. He held his champagne glass by the stem. He could even tell the brand was that old reliable Dom Pérignon and not the now hipper Cristal.

And still the boy from Cypress Bayou Trailer Park of Lafayette, Louisiana, lurked inside him. Inescapable. Maybe even necessary.

All in all, he'd much rather snag that hot blonde in the red dress, a bottle of whiskey and head home.

Even as he managed not to choke over yet another story about hunting lodges and the advantages of buying a personal Learjet, he watched her. He smiled internally as she accepted a breath mint from her dark-haired friend. His body tightened as she snitched a chocolate truffle from a tray of sweets and slid it into her mouth with a sigh of pleasure, her tongue peeking out to skim the last drop of chocolate from her bottom lip. He noticed as she slipped into the kitchen, then return moments later with a large silver platter of strawberries.

At first glance, he'd pegged her as a guest. With her

sparkling dress; tall, trim body; and sleek curtain of hair falling just past her shoulders, she had class written all over her. But when he'd maneuvered himself closer, he saw her nails were painted bloodred, and she had a small butterfly tattoo on the back of her left shoulder.

And he'd smiled genuinely for the first time all night.

Now, while a local cardiologist—whom his company was panting over as a client to represent in nuisance malpractice suits—explained the advantages of jetting to Brussels in the spring, he watched the chocolate-loving blonde rearrange strawberries on the fruit platters and considered how she'd feel about comparing body decorations.

Even as the arousing picture of that played through his mind, he strangled his libido and remembered his career. His life. His future. And the future of those who depended on him.

He'd come to Atlanta to change direction. To amend for the past. To remind himself why he'd started down the road of law in the first place.

Beautiful, butterfly-tattooed blondes would just have to wait.

He tuned into the European-vacation discussion. He smiled at appropriate times. He didn't talk too much. Or too little. And when the esteemed doctor excused himself to dance with his wife, Lucas's business card was in his jacket pocket.

With a smile, he turned to find the next conquest. But as he continued to schmooze, she was there. He felt her. Her smile and her grace. Her glowing skin. The heat her body would undoubtedly radiate.

Why couldn't he forget her? Or at least set her aside until the business of the night was done?

Nothing came before business. At least nothing ever had before.

Tonight, though, he knew where she was at every moment. He knew she hovered nearby. Lovely. Tempting. *Forbidden.*

His muscles grew tired of holding back. His fingers tingled in anticipation. He even got a crick in his neck from craning in an effort to constantly keep her in sight. For a man who'd fought for and gained control over his life and his emotions, the night was becoming both a torture and a curiosity.

Oddly enough, the moment he buckled was when he saw her holding out a tray of strawberries to an elderly couple.

After they moved away, he approached her. "I'd rather have them dipped in chocolate."

Her head jerked up, and she met his gaze with a surprised jolt, as if she'd been lost in her own thoughts.

Smart move, chère, *with this crowd.*

"They're better with a bit more sweetness," he added, somehow knowing he wasn't through giving in to temptation.

ALL THE AIR LEFT Vanessa's body.

She shook her head to clear it, certain she was hallucinating.

A tall, trim, black-haired, green-eyed, strong-jawed, impeccably dressed vision of a man was *not* standing in front of her. Popping out while she was rearranging the fruit.

Quick, girl. Think of something clever. Knock that hard head of yours against something if necessary.

Instead, she stared.

His smile was just a tad too confident, but his eyes were bright, as if lit from within. His posture and broad shoulders communicated assurance and reliability, giving her the impression that he was capable of slaying dragons, should such a drastic measure be necessary. She noted the crystal champagne flute in his hand, and the Rolex encircling his wrist, completing the picture of powerful elegance.

Why him? Why now? she wanted to ask somebody. *Yell* at somebody. *Any*body. She was supposed to be working. Impressing the moneyed masses. Avoiding her mother's criticism. Denying her sister access to her neglected, impulsive and sometimes romantic heart. And, last but not least, mending the family fence—even if it was made of iron.

All desire for those lofty achievements had faded. Gone *poof* like a Vegas magician's assistant.

Somehow, someway, this man drew her to him, making her forget her goals and needs. Other than the most carnal ones. By self-assurance or warmth or the supernatural, she felt herself leaning closer, eager to catch the next words he said.

You're *supposed to say something,* her libido reminded her.

To stall, she glanced down to note the silver tray trembling in her hands. What had he said? Strawberries. And chocolate.

"Sweet is good," she managed to say finally, setting the

tray aside. And those impulsive, rebel genes, no matter how deeply buried, popped out like a stripper's implants. She stepped closer, and his eyes went hot. His subtle cologne and body heat enveloped her. "Tasty. Tart. Warm."

"Exactly," he said, his voice barely more than a whisper.

Desire slid through her body. When she'd first gotten out on her own, she'd picked up a few guys at bars, just to give her cramped wings a stretch, but her social life had quickly taken a backseat to work. The success of her business was vital to her wallet, her peace of mind and her pride. She hadn't met a guy who could hold her admittedly short attention span for very long.

But her attention was riveted now. "I have strawberries just for the chocolate." She licked her lips. "Do you need a demonstration on how to dip them?"

"Love one."

She turned away, leading him to the chocolate fountain. Now that she wasn't facing him, she could think a bit clearer. She thanked heaven, her lucky stars and her fairy godmother that she'd seen him before Mia. Friends they were, but *wow*, he would be hard to be friendly about.

When they reached the table, she felt the tip of his finger skim her shoulder. "I like the butterfly," he said.

The warmth of his touch lingered on her skin, and she shivered as she glanced back at him. "Glad somebody does. My mother—" She had *not* just brought her mother into a discussion with Mr. Delectable. Mortification burned her face.

Those wicked green eyes twinkled. "Mine, too."

"*You* have a tattoo? I thought Rolex cross-checked that

sort of behavior before they let just anybody waltz around with their goods."

He raised his eyebrows. "The tattoo came first."

Damn. Another flub. He probably thought she was one of those gold-digging chicks who checked out the labels in a guy's clothes before she tried to hook her claws into him. "What is it?" she asked in an attempt to recover.

"And here I thought you'd wanna know *where* before *what*," he said, his voice low and seductive.

He even had a nice accent. Southern, but smooth. Not good ol' boy and not suppressed as if he'd taken classes on how to lose his heritage like so many she knew. "Maybe you could show me instead."

His finger trailed down her arm. "Not here I couldn't."

Oh, my. She swallowed. "Somewhere more private?"

"You don't have to work?"

"Yes. No."

Yes, you do, her conscience reminded her. *Work, smirk,* her libido countered.

"I've got a few minutes," she said coolly, though it was hard to be cool when one's knees were on the verge of buckling beneath the weight of Mr. Wonderful's interested stare.

"To spend with me?"

"If you like."

"You're good at your job." His gaze roved her face. "I watched you. For quite a while." While her breath hitched in her throat, he glanced around before his gaze came back to hers. "The food is excellent. The layout and decorations shine with class. The guests…" He shrugged as he snagged two glasses of champagne from the passing waiter, then handed her one.

Though she didn't normally drink her clients' liquor, she sipped and couldn't stop the eye roll for the guests.

He grinned. "A bit tedious?"

"A bit."

"Self-importance tends to make the air thick."

"I knew I was short of breath for a reason." Though she very well knew the real reason. "Ninety percent of them are doctors and lawyers. Arrogance is a job qualification." She started to smile again, but the amused expression on his face tipped her off to her blunder. Only occasionally had she paid attention during etiquette lessons. "Which one are you?"

He toasted her with his flute. "Lawyer."

"Not around here." No way this guy could have flown under the gossip radar, even if she was on the outer edges of the circle.

"I am as of Monday."

She hadn't heard this. She wondered if he'd be working with her father or rivaling him. Regret rolled over her. Why a lawyer? That hit too close to home. A home where she was no longer welcome. "Congratulations," she said without any warmth.

"Don't like lawyers?" He sipped. "Pity. I was looking forward to that chocolate-dipping demonstration."

Glancing at him, at the interest, the regret in his eyes, she waved aside the old prejudice. And the memory of guys who'd used her to get close to her father. The pain of rejection she couldn't seem to shake.

Thanks to the man before her, desire and curiosity

had woven their spell, dispelling her conscience's shouts of caution.

She turned to pick up a wooden skewer, slid a strawberry onto the end, then rolled it beneath the warm chocolate spilling from a spout on the fountain. The seductive, sugary aroma surrounded her like a lover, lulling her in its warm embrace. Mischievous thrills zipped down her spine.

An elderly couple approached and took their sweet time selecting a crystal plate and fruit, drenching it in chocolate, smiling at each other the whole time. Vanessa had seen the same effect on many people over the past few years. There was just something plain decadent about chocolate. Liquefy the stuff? Oh, boy. The sparks will fly.

With her own sparks ready to ignite, she turned.

Knowing she should take a cautious look around, but ignoring the call to respectability, she cupped her hand under the dripping strawberry and held it in front of his lips.

He turned his head. "Lose the skewer."

She hesitated. She was a rebel, not a troublemaker. Most of the time anyway.

"Come on," he added.

Hardly able to believe she was complying in a room filled with her parents and all their respected cronies, but unable to resist his dare, she slid the dripping strawberry off the skewer and held it between her fingers, against his mouth. His gaze never leaving hers, he bit in, his tongue catching the tip of her finger. The juices flowed over her fingers, dripping into her palm. Her body tingled; her stomach fluttered.

She wanted him. Wanted him like crazy.

Heart hammering, she popped the rest of the berry in her mouth, then chased the sweetness with champagne. As the icy drink rolled down her throat, she wiped her hand on a napkin and tried to find some balance, some reason to resist him. And came up flat empty.

"How fast can you get out of here?" he asked, setting aside his glass.

"I—" She put down her glass. "This is nuts. I don't even know your name."

"Lucas."

"Is that first or last?"

"First. That's enough for now, isn't it? I'm tired of networking and dropping names to impress. I don't want to compare stationery or brag about judgments and client lists."

For a second, she was shocked by the naughty "first names only" suggestion. But it also appealed to her on a couple of levels.

First, it was naughty.

Second, if he learned her last name, he'd most likely connect her with her father. How many guys had she gone out with at her mother or sister's suggestion, only to learn they were aspiring attorneys looking to break into her father's firm?

"And your name?" her gorgeous companion asked.

Her mother would probably have a stroke if she found out her daughter had picked up a man—*a stranger*—at her dignified children's hospital fund-raiser. Her sister would demand lineage and financial-status reports. Her father would want to see his law degree and standing with the American Bar Association.

Really, discretion was in order.

And yet she itched—in more places than just her brain—to take a chance. To plunge and then dive. To walk down an expected road and see where it led. She was literally on the edge of jumping in with both feet and not asking too many questions.

So she did. Ask a question, that is.

"Do you have a fiancée?"

He angled his head. "No."

"A wife?"

He grinned. "No."

She tapped her foot.

Then again, picking up a guy at a party would be a scandalous—and honest—way of telling her sister she was dating. Lately, she'd been assuring her matchmaking-minded sibling that she had all the dates she needed. Not *exactly* a lie. She just didn't *need* any dates at the moment.

Mr. Scrumptious, however, could easily change her mind. She glanced up at him. And smiled.

"Vanessa," she said, sliding her hand across the lapel of his suit jacket. "My name's Vanessa."

2

SHE WAS A CONTRADICTION.

Manners, but flaunted tradition. Elegant, but proudly sported a tattoo. Vanessa had cued in on his Rolex, but didn't seem moved by the moneyed crowd.

A puzzle Lucas would like to solve. Later, much later.

Even though he stepped outside into the blast of a humid summer night, the heat couldn't match the fire coursing through him. He could still feel the brush of her hand against his chest. Instead of the sweet scent of the magnolia trees dotting the country-club lawn, he smelled her alluring Asian-spice perfume.

As much as he valued the control he'd gained over his life and his actions, he'd only narrowly resisted yanking her against himself and kissing her until neither of them could breathe. Forget networking. Reputations and decorum be damned.

For the first time in a long, great while, the thrill of the hunt had taken over but had nothing to do with his career.

When his senses seized him, so did the memories. He longed for the cigarettes he'd given up, since trips into the past didn't come without ghosts. Wandering past manicured flower beds behind a posh Atlanta country club, he instead remembered the scent of chicory, fish fresh from the stream, Spanish moss dripping like tattered lacy curtains over the swamp. He recalled friends he'd partied with in New Orleans, the small knot of family he'd left behind and crawfish boils shared with both—the potatoes, onions and dark red crustaceans spilling out across a newspaper-lined folding table, while the music heated up and whiskey cooled the fire.

Louisiana would always be in his blood, he supposed, even if sometimes he wanted to exorcise it from his mind.

And here, on the outside, beyond the windows where the thoroughbreds looked out into the mundane, with his past shimmering in his blood, seemed the perfect place to wait for Vanessa. When the party was over, they would continue what they'd started.

He justified his exit from party networking by reminding himself he was mostly a mystery to the people inside, and it wouldn't be wise to push himself too firmly just yet. His change of heart and legal specialty wouldn't be welcomed by some, wouldn't be believed by others. Keeping his distance, allowing them to learn about him in pieces, and, of course, letting the rumors fester and grow more elaborate could only help.

For years he'd deliberately kept the details of his past sketchy. Having a shady cousin who specialized in security matters worked in his favor at times. Some of his history they would never learn—or understand—but that also had its advantages. In his new life he wanted to walk in the light. He was tired of wading through muck, even though he always managed to find the gold in places nobody else wanted to go.

A talent or a curse?

He wasn't sure he cared anymore. At least the money he'd earned had its uses. It provided comfort and security where once he'd suffered misery and chaos.

He heard the stumbling shuffle behind him before he turned and saw the heavyset man coming down the path. He guessed his age at under twenty-five, possibly a former athlete who'd stopped intense training and taken up late-night steak dinners and bourbon.

"Hallooo!" the guy said as he waved—and weaved—drunkenly toward Lucas.

Damn it to hell. I don't have time for this.

"Bea-u-ti-ful night, ya think?" the drunk guy mumbled, gesturing with the crystal tumbler in his right hand.

"Ou—" Lucas had to physically stop the Cajun French from leaking out. "Yes."

"I tell ya." The man clapped a friendly hand on Lucas's shoulder. "I haven't seen a night like this 'un since our big hunt of oh-two. We were stalking these turkeys…"

Please, dear God, not another hunting story.

"Fascinating," Lucas cut in. "Are you a profession-al?" From experience, he knew hunters loved this mistaken assumption.

Sure enough, the guy's chest puffed out. "Nah. Just do it on trips with the firm."

"What firm?" Lucas asked casually.

If possible, his chest expanded more. "Douglas and Al-derman."

"Ah. Top drawer."

"You bet yer ass."

For a moment, Lucas wondered if the guy talked with

that heavy slang at the office. He couldn't imagine so. Douglas and Alderman were reportedly both a couple of old-moneyed curmudgeons, who brandished traditionalism, dignity and family pedigrees like swords.

"'Course he's gone and done it now."

"Who?"

"Broke the code."

Lucas angled his head as the guy took another long swallow from his glass. "Who broke what code?"

"Douglas. Joseph freakin' Douglas."

Ah. The premier curmudgeon. Who certainly wouldn't want to be gossiped about by a junior executive. Which this guy had to be.

Lucas fought against curiosity and ethics. The latter he'd given up some time ago, and now wanted back. He should excuse himself. Hell, he should run the other way.

He didn't move.

Though he'd never had the pleasure of a face-to-face introduction with Douglas, earlier that evening he'd not-so-subtly steered his elegant wife in the opposite direction from Lucas and the circle of people he had been talking to. They were undoubtedly part of the crowd who would likely never accept Lucas's change of specialty. Of course, his lineage didn't include Civil War generals whose wife and children had held their ground against Union troops in front of the family's plantation home, then served them fried chicken, turnip greens and biscuits until peace was declared, thereby saving one of the few seventeenth-century homes still standing in Atlanta.

By contrast, Lucas's ancestors had probably been too

busy helping Blackbeard and Jean Lafitte pirate and profit in the Big Easy to bother with turnip greens.

He wondered if Douglas's dissing could be an effort at intimidation. It likely wasn't personal; he probably just didn't like competition. Douglas's firm had a division that specialized in helping companies and hospitals protect themselves against frivolous lawsuits—exactly the job Lucas had just been hired to do by Geegan, Duluth and Patterson.

"I couldn't believe it," the drunk guy muttered, hanging his head. "Ya can't have two wills. Ya just can't."

Despite his effort not to listen, Lucas's legal antenna shot up. "No. You certainly can't."

"Mrs. Switzer, she's so nice. She's so broke. It's not right. We have to help her."

"Of course you do."

"But it's still not right. The other will, you know."

"The other will?"

"The one Mr. Switzer had Mr. Douglas draw up last month, just before he died. Why did he have to even talk to that stripper? And in Daytona Beach?"

"His client drew up another will?"

"No." He shook his head emphatically, then laid his finger against his lips. "It's a secret. Mrs. Switzer's so nice. Did I tell you she always calls me by name? She always says, 'Good morning, Anthony, how are you today?' in that soft voice."

"How gracious of her."

"Mr. Switzer shouldn't have had that affair. Mrs. Switzer's so nice."

He definitely should have run, Lucas reflected. There

was a time when he would have relished having this kind of information about a competitor or opposing attorney. Other people's bad habits—and subsequent carelessness—had fueled more than one victory in his past.

A stripper, an affair, illegally ignoring a client's wishes? *Two* wills? It was an orgy of scandal.

He eyed the drunk junior executive next to him. Maybe the guy was full of crap. He could have gotten Douglas mixed up with an episode of *Law & Order* for all he knew.

He clapped the guy on the shoulder, then walked by him. "Sorry to hear about your troubles, *mon ami,* but I've got a hot date."

"Hey, ya never tol' me your name, buddy!"

Even if he had, the guy likely wouldn't remember it. But Lucas couldn't take the chance regardless. "No, I didn't, did I?"

He inclined his head, then headed inside through the kitchen door.

"HOW HOT?" MIA ASKED, her eyes blazing with excitement.

"Smokin'," Vanessa assured her as she stacked dirty dishes in a storage box.

"Ooh, you get all the good ones!"

Vanessa cut her gaze to her friend. "I do not. You do."

Mia grinned. "Oh, right."

"You get all the good ones, play with them awhile, then toss them away like old socks."

"Somebody has to try them out and warn the rest of you away."

"Half those guys want to marry you."

Mia wrinkled her nose. "Exactly my point. Yuck."

Vanessa shook her head and finished loading the box. Mia's mother had been married and divorced four—or was it five?—times, so, not surprisingly, Mia considered matrimony as the black hole of relationships. *She's happy until that "I do, you do, we do" business,* Mia always said, *then dullsville becomes splitsville. No thank you.*

Vanessa just hoped her friend wasn't playing the breakup game because she was afraid she'd follow in her mother's footsteps.

Oh, like you aren't afraid of following in your mother's footsteps? Red bra, tattoo and attitude—you're a walking case of fear of debutante-itis.

Vanessa mentally waved away her bothersome conscience. "Still, Mia, you need to find a boyfriend. Somebody you love. Or can at least date for more than a month."

"Why?"

Good question. She wasn't sure. Maybe it was this longing to reconnect with her family that had her wishing for a lasting relationship in her life. In the past, when things hadn't worked out with a guy, she'd shrugged and moved on, but lately she found herself wondering if she should consider her choices more carefully, if she should slow down and look for a more serious relationship.

Mia grinned. "Remember that great line by Madeline Kahn in *Clue*? Something about how men should be like tissues—"

"*Soft, strong and disposable.* I remember, but she didn't have Colin—"

"Out." Mia waggled her hands in a shooing motion. "Go find Mr. Hot. I'll finish up."

The reminder of Lucas brought a wave of longing and heat sizzled through her body. She was being brazen and rebellious again, flitting off into the night with a man she'd met just an hour ago. A man whose last name she didn't even know. A man who would no doubt turn out to be mistake number 423.

She'd slow down tomorrow.

All but vibrating on the spot, she asked Mia, "Are you sure there's not too much to clean up alone?"

"I'll get Colin to help."

"Good idea. I'll call you later."

"I'm jealous."

"I know."

"And he's even safe. That ridiculous brandishing your invitation and a picture ID business your mother insisted on actually worked out in your favor."

Her mother *was* the overprotective type, which is exactly why neither she, nor Vanessa, could classify what she was doing as safe. "He could be a closet fetishist. Maybe he likes to wear women's underwear."

"Or he could be bad in bed."

Vanessa laid the back of her hand across her forehead. "Perish the thought."

"Seriously, drive your own car, keep your purse, your Mace and your cell phone nearby." Mia bit her lip. "Maybe I should meet him…. You know, just to be sure I get good vibes, too."

No woman in their right mind would want a potential lover to meet gorgeous, darkly sultry Mia. Vanessa blew her a kiss as she backed toward the door. "I'm fine, and you're too good to me."

"It's a big sacrifice, all right."

"Be nice to Colin."

"Yeah, yeah."

Before Vanessa could do more than smile, the door at her back swung open. She spun and found herself face-to-face with Lucas.

His broad shoulders almost completely filled the doorway. In the bright light of the kitchen, she could see the custom-made details of his dark blue suit and perfectly pressed white shirt. His hair was windblown into sexy disarray. His eyes, seeming even more intensely green than she remembered them, focused on her face. When a hint of his spicy cologne floated toward her, her knees wobbled.

As she grappled for stability in a world suddenly wavering, she tried to focus on what it was about him that riveted her attention.

His amazing looks, certainly. His elegance, intelligence and confidence, too.

But there was more. A kindred, tattooed spirit? A risk-taking nature? A sense that he, too, felt alone in the world much of the time? Hadn't she just been wondering why she always had to be the pursuer in her relationships? Hadn't she just told herself she'd give away a prized cheesecake recipe to have a man look at her the way Colin did Mia?

Well, here certainly was a man pursuing her and looking at her with more than a casual interest....

That look was it. Or part of it.

He *focused* on her. Only her. As if no one else existed for miles. The desire to continue to be the center of his attention was overwhelming her, drawing her closer to him as if he had a magnet buried inside his chest.

One side of his mouth turned up in an enigmatic smile. "Just the woman I was looking for." His gaze slid to Mia, then back to Vanessa. "Ready to go?"

As her heart fluttered, she somehow managed to keep her voice from trembling. "Lucas, this is my roommate and business partner, Mia Medini. Mia, Lucas..."

"Broussard," he filled in, giving Vanessa a wink that told her he wasn't afraid of his last name.

Unlike her.

Lucas approached Mia with his hand outstretched.

Mia's eyes widened briefly before she shook his hand. "Nice to meet you."

"You ladies did a wonderful job with the party." His gaze met Vanessa's. "I especially liked the strawberries...and chocolate."

Vanessa's stomach trembled.

And it happened again. He looked at her as if nobody else were there. His eyes glittered with the promise of delight and pleasure.

And, except for that light stroke against my tattoo, he hasn't even touched me.

"You should try her double-chocolate cheesecake," Mia inserted into the charged silence.

Lucas raised his eyebrows, the way Vanessa remembered him doing when they'd talked about his tattoo. "I'll be sure to have a taste."

Just one? she longed to ask and no doubt would have

if her roommie hadn't been standing so close. "We should probably get going. Are you sure you're okay?" she asked Mia.

"I'm fine." She waggled her finger at Lucas. "You take care of my buddy."

"I promise, *chère*."

Chère? He spoke French? With a name like Broussard, he could be French. But then there was that Southern accent. Maybe he was from New Orleans. Growing up, she'd been to several charity balls down there. Her father loved the tradition and genteel manners of the Creoles.

What if my parents could actually like this one as much as I do?

But she immediately dismissed the idea. She'd known the man an hour and she was considering introducing him to her parents? No. Forget it.

This night was about desire. Chemistry. Carnal exploration. There wasn't a future for a party pickup.

A group of servers strode into the kitchen carrying dirty dishes and glasses. Still feeling a bit guilty about leaving Mia, but not about to lose her opportunity with Mr. Beautiful, Vanessa grabbed her purse and keys, then slipped out the back door with Lucas.

"Your friend Mia is worried about you," he said as they walked toward the parking lot.

Distracted by the deep timbre of his voice and the occasional brush of his shoulder against hers, Vanessa nodded, then shook her head. "She's just jealous."

"That you get to leave without cleaning up?"

"That I get to leave with you."

"We could invite her along."

Great. He's into orgies. You can really pick 'em, Vanessa. "One woman's not enough for you?"

"You're definitely enough. But if you need a chaperone…"

She glanced at him and wished she hadn't. His smile made her hot and light-headed. Thankfully, though the day's humidity hadn't dissipated much, a breeze chose that moment to gather enough strength to graze her skin. "I'll pass."

"If you insist."

Was he kidding or was that part of his sharp humor? She wanted to get to know his brain almost as much as his body. Pausing at the back of her car, she commented, "Mia's very beautiful, don't you think?"

He stepped close, brushing a strand of her hair off her cheek. "Is she?"

Though all the air left her body at his proximity and her stomach quivered at his touch, she said coolly, "You're trying to flatter me."

"Of course. Is it working?"

"Of course. Is it because you want to get me into bed?"

He smiled. "Certainly."

Dear heaven, he was temptation incarnate. And he was taking control of her senses with simple words and bare brushes against her skin. "I'm driving my car," she said, needing to find some sense of practicality with the wild step she was taking.

"Okay."

"I don't doubt your driving skills or anything. I just want to have my own car. I mean I hardly know you, and—"

"I might turn out to be a guy who likes to wear women's underwear."

"Exactly."

Staring up at him, the lure of attraction dragged her closer—not that she was fighting too hard anyway. A fog of need and curiosity had wrapped itself around her the moment she'd seen him. If she turned on a bright light, she might dispel the aura of mystery surrounding him. But she had no intention of doing so.

She'd fallen into a fantasy. And she liked it there.

"Can I have your cell-phone number in case we get separated?" he asked, all polite manners, even as she was igniting from the inside.

She gave it to him as he opened her door. "Where are we going?"

"My place." Then he stepped forward, his face hovering less than an inch from hers. She could feel his breath on her skin, see the hunger in his eyes as his gaze dropped to her lips.

She wanted him to crush her against his chest. She wanted his mouth on hers, his body vibrating with the same need as hers.

But he just lightly pressed his lips to hers. The simple touch reverberated all the way to her toes. She inhaled the spicy scent of him, braced her hands against his waist.

He cupped her face as he pulled back. "You'll follow me?"

Anywhere you want to go, baby. She cleared her throat and resisted yanking him against her lips. "Yes. I— Sure."

"You're nervous?"

She was a lot of things, but nervous wasn't one of them. "No."

"I am." With that, he drew his fingertip along her jaw, then retreated. "I'll pull my car around."

Shaking from the inside out, Vanessa could do little more than nod. The man had amazing...presence.

By the time they'd driven away from the country club, she'd managed to rein in her hormones enough that she no longer feared spontaneous combustion. No doubt temporarily, but still that was something.

He wanted her. She could all but see the attraction shimmering between them. Yet he remained smooth. Composed. In control. Maybe he'd give her lessons.

After they'd driven a few miles away from the quiet elegance of moneyed homes, past the tall towers of office buildings and heading toward midtown, her cell phone rang.

"I haven't thought about, looked at or considered any other woman since the moment I saw you."

"We just met an hour ago."

He laughed. "I really do like you, Vanessa."

"Which brings up a good point. I know your last name. You don't know mine."

"Do you want to tell me?" he asked, his voice echoing intimately in her ear.

"Not particularly."

"Then don't."

"How much farther?"

"We're nearly there."

"You live in midtown?"

"My office is nearby. It's convenient."

She wanted to ask about his office but didn't. Her

father's office was also nearby, but he certainly would have mentioned hiring an old-moneyed Louisiana lawyer, which Lucas had to be, so he must work for a rival firm. In her father's eyes, *every* firm was a rival, after all.

For a moment—a really brief moment—she considered turning off. He was part of the world she'd left a long time ago, a world she'd honestly never felt comfortable living in. Did she really want to get involved with a man who did? Despite the few times she'd given in to her sister's setups, she'd been careful not to fish from her old pond.

Involved? You're not getting involved. Carnal exploration, heat, falling into a fantasy. That's it, remember?

Her pulse skipped a beat as she pictured the heated look in Lucas's eyes.

Oh, I remember.

They pulled into the parking lot of a luxury high-rise apartment building. Vanessa's hands trembled as she shut off her car. They barely spoke as they rode in the elevator to the sixteenth floor.

Lucas rested his hand at the small of her back, and they watched the numbers light in amber sequence. Sometime during the drive he'd ditched his tie and unbuttoned his shirt. Vanessa fought the urge to slide her hand in the opening and see if his chest was as warm and hard as she'd imagined. By the time sixteen dinged, her palms were sweating.

He unlocked the door to his apartment, tossed his keys on a mahogany table in the foyer, and before she could do more than glimpse at the sunken living room decorated in neutral shades, he'd pinned her to the wall.

"Wanna throw down right here?"

Instinctively, she arched into her body against his. *Finally* was all she could think. Finally his composure had snapped. She wasn't alone. He, too, felt this clawing, aching need. This desire that throbbed through her like a second pulse.

She had the sense that grabbing him—or, hell, just nodding at him—would be enough to have him ripping off their clothes and driving himself deep inside her. She wanted that immediate gratification. It would keep her from questioning her decision. It would keep things simple. She wanted him. She was drawn to him and intrigued by him. Did she really need to *know* him?

Before she could form an answer, he slid his hand gently across her cheek, then stepped back. "Relax, *chère,* I have some manners."

Still trying to catch her breath, she stared after him for a stunned and confused—and needy—minute before curiosity forced her to follow him down the hall and into the kitchen, which was as sophisticated and sleek as he was. Black marble countertops, gleaming appliances, ceramic-tile floor and iron stools lined up along a curved bar.

What was with the manners thing? *Some* manners? He was impeccable. She'd spent a lifetime trying and failing to be that smooth.

He was a bit forward, she supposed, but for some reason, she doubted he came on to every woman the way he had her. Something about her had set him off. Just as the same had happened to her. She felt a connection to him she didn't even feel in the presence of her own family. But when he wasn't touching her, or looking at her in that intimate way he had, he seemed like a stranger.

He is.

He opened a below-the-counter wine fridge and pulled out a bottle. "I'm having whiskey, but I imagine you'd like something a bit softer."

Was she predictable now? And soft? In her mind, *soft* was just another word for gentle, quiet or—worse—demure.

Oh, hell no.

She could admit to herself she was questioning her impulse to leave with him. She could silently acknowledge she was uncertain and off balance. But she wasn't about to let him in on those weaknesses.

She was strong. Self-possessed. Bold. Confident.

She'd worked her ass off to make sure.

Leaning one hip against the counter, she said, "I'll have whiskey."

In the process of retrieving a wineglass from the cabinet, he turned. "One finger or two?"

Oh, God, she was pretty sure that meant straight. No ice, no mixer. She swallowed bravely, then smiled at the challenge in his eyes. "Whatever you're having."

He set two crystal tumblers on the counter, then poured a healthy amount into each from a bottle of Jack Daniel's. Black Label. He handed one to her, then raised his glass. "To tattoos."

She tapped her glass against his. "And chocolate." She sipped and felt heroic when she managed to down a swallow of the burning liquid without choking.

"Good?" he asked, raising one cocky eyebrow.

She actually liked the taste of whiskey; she just didn't like swallowing it. She'd dated a saxophone player once who'd always sipped whiskey at the end of his set, and he'd tasted fabulous. Drinking the stuff, though—especially without ice—must be an acquired thing.

"Smooth," she managed to say.

"After the third or fourth glass, you hardly taste it at all."

Now her chest was burning. "I'm sure."

Grinning as if he knew the torture she was enduring, he linked hands with her and led her down the steps, through the living room and onto the balcony.

Though the view of the sparkling sky was stunning, and the balcony was nearly as richly decorated as the inside, Vanessa wasn't sure they could accomplish the night's goal on the wicker couch and chaise longue. But Lucas leaned against the balcony wall, the lights from the high-rise across the street framing his body, as if he planned to hang out there all night.

"You have a thing about being outside, don't you?" she asked.

"The fresh air clears my mind—" he toasted her "—which you've fogged up quite nicely."

Bravely, Vanessa took another sip of her whiskey. "And you need a clear head?"

"Yes."

"What happens if you don't have one?"

"I grab you and drag you back to my bedroom."

Sounds pretty good to me. "And you don't want to do that because…"

"I want to too much."

Is it any wonder I'm fascinated with the man? "What happens to things you want too much?"

"I still get them. I'm just not especially gracious—or gentle—about the process."

Oh my.

There was certainly more to Lucas than his steaming sensuality and good looks. He wasn't just a corporate lawyer in a slick suit. Away from the rich and powerful crowd where he'd both blended in and stood out, his allure only grew stronger, the mystery of where he'd come from only deepened.

Vanessa set her glass on the ledge and stepped closer to him. "You're trying to warn me off."

"I'm not. At all."

"But you're deliberately acting dark and mysterious."

"I *am* dark and mysterious."

"Ha! You're an open book."

"No kidding."

"You're from Louisiana," she began, watching his eyes widen as she obviously hit the mark. "I'm thinking New Orleans. The place is steeped in Creole history. The family homestead is probably in the Garden District. Your grandmother would be the matriarch—as is proper in all of New Orleans society. There's a scandal in your family's past, probably something to do with a riverboat gambler or pirate. I'm betting the family money started in agriculture—rice or sugarcane probably—but at some point somebody wise invested in manufacturing or real estate. And you, since you have a bit of the rebel in you, decided not to toe the family line completely and studied law. At Tulane, I'm sure. Where you didn't pledge the proper fraternity, but instead bought a motorcycle and got a tattoo. With your wild days behind you after law school, you went into a well-established practice back home. But after a while you decided you needed a new challenge and came here. Where I found you, being bored to smithereens by the hunting stories and name dropping of the Atlanta Country Club." She paused and studied his blank expression with interest. "Pretty close, huh?"

Roaring with laughter, he hooked his arm around her waist, pulling her against him.

"I'm right, aren't I?"

His body continued to shake. "Absolutely. One hundred percent. That last observation was dead-on."

She laid her hands against his chest and glared up at him. "Why do I have the feeling I'm more wrong than right?"

"Mmm." He smiled broadly. "Well, let's just say I'm not going to ask you to read a jury anytime soon."

It was the smile that did it.

Her annoyance fell away. He was even more beautiful when he smiled. All he had to do was touch her, and suddenly she wasn't quite so interested in her story as she was in the feel of his body against hers. The magic they generated. The warmth emanating from his skin. The spicy scent of his cologne.

His throat, just at eye level, begged for her touch. His lips, no doubt sweet and smoky from the drink, glistened. His erection, pressing against his pants, certainly had its own pleasurable agenda.

He tossed back the rest of his whiskey, then set his glass aside and didn't make a move to get more. She could already taste him on her tongue.

With charm, money and looks like his, he was undoubtedly used to women throwing themselves at him. She was certainly one in a long line. But she didn't care.

She had a package of condoms in her purse.

"I like the taste of whiskey better like this," she said, then she cupped the back of his head and pulled him toward her waiting mouth.

3

As Vanessa's tongue slid past his lips, Lucas pulled her hard against his chest, barely able to believe he finally had her alone. She at his mercy; he at hers.

She was glorious and beautiful. Smart and funny. Sexy and sassy. She tested his hard-won control, pushing him to impatience and recklessness. He'd overcome those weaknesses. He had to remember he'd moved beyond his ugly past. Though the intensity of his need for her scared him, he had no intention of turning back. Probably couldn't even if he wanted to.

He wondered if she'd ever dreamed about the man she'd just described. He wondered if she cared about his money—or how he'd made it.

One night would never be enough, he knew that now, even if he'd tried to deny it when he'd first seen her. But when morning came, when she learned about him as he wanted to know her, would she understand? Or would she snub him?

Somehow, he didn't think snubbing was in her. Certainly not because she was the hired help—she hadn't started life that way. She'd bought his veneer of sophistication, as many had before, so she recognized the type of person he'd become. Without a doubt, there was a trust fund in her past. Maybe she was a caterer due to passion or hard times, but he had no doubt he'd find blue blood if she cut her finger.

Unlike the lovely Vanessa, he knew how to read people. And read them well.

He wondered whether she'd laugh or recoil if she knew how he'd become successful. He wondered if she'd appreciate or pull away from his need for control. Inevitably, he also considered whether she'd tangle her tongue with his quite so enthusiastically if she knew his true story. His true self.

"Nervous?" she asked as she pulled back with a gasp.

His gaze locked on her lips. He wanted them on his again. Had to have them. Had to have *her*.

And she wanted to *talk*.

She doesn't know you. The whispered words of his conscience fought their way through his baser desires. Women—even a lovely rebel in a red dress—needed connections. He had to listen to the instincts that had served him well for so many years.

Making an effort to focus, he cupped her backside, pulling her tight against his erection. "No, I'm not nervous." *I'm dying.*

Her gaze searching his, she gripped the back of his neck. "But you were."

Vaguely, he remembered telling her that just before they'd left the country-club parking lot. A lapse, he realized now, though at the time he'd simply been trying to put her at ease. She'd been understandably uncomfortable about leaving with a stranger, and he'd wanted her to know his own nerves weren't quite so calm.

Because I wanted you to like me.

He could hardly say that. Admitting a weakness, as he'd learned many times in the past, was always a mistake. "I'm not now." Rubbing his thumb across her bottom lip, he added, "Let me show you."

He trailed kisses along her jaw, reveling in the softness of her skin, inhaling the seductive aroma of strawberries and chocolate. Was that scent in his head, or did she really smell so sweet?

He fought the building tide of need coursing through his body, the ache that started between his legs and shimmered outward in waves of trembling desire. He'd made himself into something more than trailer-park trash, and he intended to prove it.

Slow down. Seduce her gently.

If he aroused her with enough skill, she wouldn't think clearly enough to question their chemistry, to wonder if she might be making a mistake. He didn't want her to think and question. He wanted the openness he'd sensed in her from the beginning.

He wanted her hot. Needy. Panting.

He flicked his tongue over her earlobe, and she gasped.

Mmm...progress.

"What, what are you feeling now?" she asked, her breath hitching.

"Hard." He scraped his teeth against the soft skin behind her ear. "Impatient."

More than impatient. He wanted to drown in her, to forget the past and the future. His need for her touch, her sighs of pleasure, had become vital.

Her hands slid down his chest, her fingers curling into

his shirt. "I want you, Lucas." She slid her thigh between his legs, pressing up against his hardness. "I probably shouldn't, but I do."

His erection pulsed almost to the point of pain. Having her was a compulsion, a mission that *must* succeed. The sugary scent of her surrounded him, enveloping him in a fog of lust so acute his world had narrowed only to her face and the warmth and pleasure her body offered.

He cupped the back of her neck. Her eyes glittered with hunger as she stared back at him. "You should." Angling his head, he covered her mouth with his.

Dive. Drown. Never surface.

As he swept his tongue into her mouth, she kneaded his shirt in her fist and rolled her hips, the warmth between her legs heating his thigh.

He turned, leaning against the balcony wall, making sure she still straddled his thigh. She rubbed herself against him, a moan and gasp escaping her lips when their mouths parted. He could only imagine the flesh scraping his leg, but he knew he wanted a taste.

He slid his hands down her back, across her enticingly curvy butt, down to the hem of her racy red dress—which he bunched in his hands, then raised. When he encountered the miniscule thong panty beneath her clothes, he nearly dropped to his knees. He should have expected such freedom from his impulsive, tattooed caterer, but that didn't lessen the jolt of erotic heat that hit him, knowing so much naked flesh lay barely concealed by her dress.

Trailing his lips over her chin and down her throat, he kneaded her bare skin and felt a shiver sweep her body, exposed to the night air.

Fast losing control, but knowing he had to hold on, he suppressed the desire to rip away her miniscule panties and drive himself into her tight, wet warmth. To assuage the hunger pulsing through him. Still, he *had* to touch her.

He hooked his thumbs beneath the seam of her panties.

She moaned.

And he smiled.

Moving around her hip bones, he slid his index finger slowly, deliberately toward the juncture of her thighs, the coarse hairs covering her sex teasing him. He let his finger dip briefly into the moist, soft heat.

Her breathing grew shallow, broken...needy, and he had to grit his teeth to keep from exploding on the spot. Just watching the pleasure skim across her face was its own form of torture and satisfaction.

With his other hand, he moved his palm over her bare behind, gripping the skinny thong fabric that fit between her cheeks. Holding both sides of the panties, he slid the fabric back and forth, gliding it between the lips of her sex.

"Oh, my," she gasped.

"Oh, yes."

She gripped his shoulders, then flung back her head, her long, blond hair spilling down as she let a long, low hum of need escape her lips.

Mercilessly, he worked the fabric. She rocked her hips in time to his erotic rhythm. He watched her in a fascinated daze. He'd anticipated being inside her as he brought her to the first orgasm they'd share, but he wasn't complaining. Pleasure skated across her face with obvious abandon.

He switched their positions, pinning her against the

balcony wall and hooking her leg around his waist. "Let go, lovely Vanessa," he panted in her ear as he leaned forward.

"I'm...working on it," she said, her voice hitching.

He pressed his hard cock between her legs as he dipped his head and tongued her earlobe. "We'll get naked. I'm dying to taste you." He kissed the top of her shoulder. "Everywhere."

Then, letting go of the panties, he pressed his thumb against the bare nub of flesh centered around her desire.

Her body went rigid.

He knew she hung on the precipice. Knew he had the power to send her over. "What do you want?" he rasped in her ear.

"You."

He rolled his thumb up, then down. "What do you want me to do?"

"That again."

"My pleasure." He rolled again.

"But faster."

Smiling, he complied, noting her breathing quickened, her skin flushed. Watching her, gaining wild pleasure from her pleasure, he noted the small butterfly tattoo on the back of her shoulder. He smiled, never broke his stroking rhythm and laid his lips lightly over the spot.

She exploded.

Her back arched, her eyes fluttered closed, the muscles between her legs contracted against his fingers.

Though he was still as hard as a rock, crazy satisfaction rushed through him. She was so damn beautiful.

She sagged, so he swung her into his arms and carried

her inside. She trailed her fingers through the hair at his temple. "I'm fairly sure a feminist shouldn't be carried."

"You want to walk?" he asked as he headed down the hall, his heart hammering so fast he was sure it would burst before he made it to the bed.

"Hell no. Can't stand."

Somehow chuckling in the midst of his own painful need, he strode into his bedroom. After laying her on the bed, he stripped off his shirt, then started on his pants.

She sat up suddenly, laying her hand across his crotch. "Hey there, lawman, not so fast."

"I thought you were exhausted with satisfaction."

Scooting to the edge of the bed, she tugged his belt from the loops. "Only temporarily."

He sucked in a breath of anticipation as she started on his zipper. *Hang on, man. Stay in control.*

She slid his zipper down, her fingers dipping below the band of his underwear, skimming the head of his erection.

He had the crazy image of a plane going down.

Captain, we're losing pressure. What should we do?

Hold the course.

Sorry, sir, control is outta here. You're on your own.

The moment she wrapped her hand around his rock-hard penis, his whole body went rigid. He had to close his eyes to hold on. He tried to still himself as she dragged her hand down, then up, though his knees nearly buckled. The woman was…amazing.

And if she continued to stroke him that way, he was going to completely lose it.

But he couldn't help reveling in her touch. She had a sure, confident grip. Her fingers cupped beneath the head of his penis, where she held and squeezed for a moment before stroking down again and sending his pulse soaring, his control spinning wildly.

His climax hovered, threatening and promising.

Somehow, he found the strength to grab her wrist. "I'm losing it here."

She glanced up at him, her blue eyes sparkling. "No kidding?"

Obviously, she was enjoying herself. Only fair, he supposed, since he was rapidly approaching ecstasy.

He stripped off his underwear, then leaned forward, pinning her to the mattress with his body. The feel of her against him from chest to hip was intoxicating, stimulating, somehow forbidden, even though—or maybe because—he was naked and she wasn't.

He felt dominant and predatory. As if she were his to possess and ravish.

Until she wrapped both legs around his waist.

Who's in control now? her expression seemed to scream.

In silent answer he leaned back and yanked her dress over her head in one smooth motion, leaving her wearing a lacy red bra and the matching miniscule panties. As she lay back on the bed, her wheat-colored hair spread out around her head, her gaze locked on his, he rose, standing between her legs.

Heat rolled off her. Need vibrated within him.

He laid his index finger on the top of her shoulder, then slid it down her body. Her skin glowed with sweat and gold-specked sparkles. How did women manage that? How did they find ways to glow and shine in moments of elemental need?

He paused at the front clasp of her bra and, with a flick of his fingers, popped it open. She arched her back, as if trying to press her breasts against his hand. He moved her bra aside, flicking his thumb across her nipple. She sucked in a breath and cupped her breasts, offering them to him.

Leaning forward, he dipped his head and laved her nipple with his tongue. She moaned, and he repeated the movement, teasing the tip to a hard peak. When her breathing grew labored, he straightened and slid his hand down her stomach. He liked stimulating her. He liked the needy look in her eyes. He liked…controlling her response.

A flaw maybe. But one he wasn't willing to admit to or relinquish.

He trailed his hand across her abs, then moved down, dipping his fingers beneath the waistband of her panties, just as she'd done to him.

"You've been there once. I thought it was your turn."

"It is." He bunched the panties in his fist, then jerked them down her legs. "Eventually."

But he'd been dying to taste her all night, and he certainly wasn't missing his chance.

He drew his tongue down the center of her rib cage. The teasing smell of strawberries and chocolate tracked his journey, and he knew she must wear some kind of scented lotion or perfume. Her soft, creamy skin seduced him. Her sighs encouraged him. Her body welcomed him.

When he reached her navel, he dipped his tongue in the indention. Her stomach contracted. In anticipation, he hoped.

As he slid his fingers through the hair between her

thighs, the musky scent of her essence washed over him. She was wet, her longing evident. He slid his tongue gently down her center. She clenched her thighs and sighed, but his hunger for her had been building, so he wasn't long on patience. He wanted his name on her lips, wanted to experience every part of her, absorb her inside him.

They might be virtual strangers, but she'd never forget him.

He teased her with gentle flicks, but she soon grew restless, her body jerking, her fists clenching the bedcovers, her head thrashing from side to side.

Sensing what she needed, he increased his pace, no longer teasing but bringing her the satisfaction she seemed to crave. When her hips pumped and she called his name, his body answered, his erection throbbing, demanding its pleasure.

He watched her. And his command over his body buckled.

As her pulse subsided, he scooped his pants off the floor, found a condom and rolled it on. He fitted himself between her thighs and drove inside, desperate to catch those last few contractions.

Her eyes flew open and fixed on his as she wrapped her legs around his waist. Her inner walls squeezed him.

Lucas panted so he wouldn't explode at the exquisite feel of her. He withdrew, then surged forward again, and she gripped the comforter as her hips rose to meet him.

He hadn't even turned down the sheets, he realized. Sometime between the balcony and the bedroom, he'd lost those precious manners he'd bragged about. But there was no holding back now. He didn't give a great damn about manners as sweat rolled down his back and Vanessa writhed beneath him. He increased his pace, Vanessa's hips pumping in response. His climax roared through him, and he drove harder, wanting her with him when he went over the edge. She stiffened, then pulsed hard around him.

As he collapsed on top of her, he was already planning ways to keep her, to probe her mind as well as her body and unravel the mystery as to why she'd struck him so hard, so immediately.

Right between the eyes.

"HOW ABOUT DESSERT?"

Lucas rolled to his side, propping his hand against his head. "That wasn't dessert?"

Eyes closed, her red bra parted but still on, Vanessa's lips curved in a smile. "*That* was fantastic." She paused. "But I'm still hungry."

He drew his finger down her side. Food wasn't exactly what he was hungry for, but he could be patient. "My fridge is pretty bare. I only moved in last week."

One eye cracked open. "Last week? The place is spotless. Where are the boxes, the furniture you haven't found a place for yet, the bubble wrap piled in the corners?"

"I had a service unpack everything while I was at work."

"That's...efficient."

"I don't believe in wasting time."

Her eyes popped open fully, meeting his gaze with amused satisfaction. "I kind of got that."

He liked that he could lie here with her and talk like old friends. Where was the awkwardness of strangers taking the premature leap to intimacy? Why had his desire for her increased instead of being satiated?

He ran his thumb along her bottom lip. "However…there are moments when taking your time is much more satisfying."

"Like with a soufflé?"

Completely charmed by her, he kissed her lightly. "Among others."

Wondering if her cry of hunger was mingled with a need for distance, he rolled off the bed. After sliding on a pair of jeans and a T-shirt, he walked into the bathroom and pulled his bathrobe off a hook, then laid it at the foot of the bed.

He had to make a conscious effort not to go any closer to her. She made him long to crawl into bed for a day. And even then he wasn't sure his hunger would be satisfied.

"The bathroom's all yours," he said, extending his arm toward the open French doors. "I'm sure you'll find everything you need."

She propped up on her elbows. "The service provide that, too?"

He smiled. "Of course. I'm a very good customer."

He left the bedroom and headed to the kitchen, hoping he had something that would satisfy a chocolate-loving caterer. He found cheese and grapes and a bottle of cabernet sauvignon. As he set out glasses and plates, he reflected on the fact that Vanessa Last-Name-Not-Provided was his first guest.

At some point, he'd planned to have a few key people

at the firm over for a cocktail party, but the past week had been spent immersed in learning office procedures, client lists and potential clients. This job was his first time working for someone else in nearly a decade. He needed some time to get acclimated before he hosted the partners.

When he heard the shower running, business flew from his mind. He found himself anticipating the scent of his soap on Vanessa. Her skin, soft, warm and wet from the water, he'd part the robe and kiss the side of her neck, sending her pulse racing.

She appeared at the end of the hall moments later, bundled in his robe, but a wary expression was set on her face.

Perhaps seduction should wait.

"Wine?" he asked her, holding up the bottle.

"Sure." She sat at the bar and glanced down at the plate of food. "Empty fridge, huh? I was expecting stale chips and old Chinese food."

"I was referring to my lack of chocolate. I'll have to fix that if I want to keep you around, I expect."

She selected a fat green grape. "This is great."

Noting she didn't respond to his invitation to stick around, he made the decision to keep things light, not to probe too obviously for details about her life. It would only take a simple phone call to find out the identity of the lovely blond country-club caterer.

As he slid onto the bar stool next to her, he handed her a wineglass. "Considering your exceptional skills in the kitchen, I'll take that as a compliment."

She sipped the wine, nodding with approval. "How do you like Atlanta so far?"

"It's fast. The traffic is murder."

"A bit different from New Orleans, I bet."

His hand clenched around the stem of his glass. "What makes you think I'm from New Orleans?"

She shrugged. "Earlier you called Mia *chère.* Then me, in the hall. I just figured you were from there."

He hadn't even been conscious of the endearment. A troubling thought. It made him realize how much Vanessa had affected him, distracted him. As he searched for the right answer, he took a drink. "I practiced in New Orleans, but I'm not originally from there."

"Oh, well, the accent is nice. Don't get rid of it."

"You mean like those diction classes?"

"Yeah. Pretty ridiculous."

He'd spent much of his life hating his accent, and he'd modified his speech a great deal. Only a trace remained, just enough to be identified as Southern. Just enough to appeal to a sympathetic jury. How would Vanessa feel knowing that?

Not complimentary, he was sure.

"How old are you?" she asked, choosing another grape.

"Thirty. You?"

"Twenty-seven. Did you always want to be a lawyer?"

I wanted to survive. "No. I sort of fell into it." *I got arrested.*

She held up her hand, indicating the posh apartment. "But obviously you found a niche. You're a big success. Are your parents proud?"

"My father died when I was young. My mother's proud, though." *At least when she's coherent.*

She laid her hand over his. "I'm sorry about your dad.

My father and I don't always get along, but I can't imagine being without him."

The half-truths he was telling bothered him. He wanted to be honest with her. He wanted to share his pain, his struggles. But he suspected her background was far more upstanding than his, and he wanted her too much to risk her rejection. "Did you always want to be a caterer?"

She grinned. "Not specifically. I wanted to cause trouble."

He raised his glass to her. A kindred spirit. Maybe that was part of her appeal. *"Laissez les bons temps rouler."* When she angled her head in question, he elaborated, "Let the good times roll."

"Exactly. My family has…" She glanced down at her glass, then back up to him. "They have a traditional idea of how a proper Southern lady should live her life," she continued, rolling her shoulders back. "I'm not traditional."

"That's not a crime."

"It is in my family." She sipped her wine. "Anyway, I don't mind being covered in flour, sweaty and wearing jeans. I was drawn to the fast pace of restaurants, then I got sucked in by the instant gratification—"

When he leered, she nudged him playfully with her elbow. "Gratification of *cooking*. Feed people, and for the most part, they're happy. I turned out to be a good chef." She angled her head. "I'm a *great* pastry chef, to tell you the truth."

"I know. I got a taste, remember?"

She licked her lips. "I remember." Her hand danced toward the plate, then she drew back. Her gaze locked with his. "I'm sometimes impulsive to my own detriment."

"Like tonight?"

"No. Yes. I don't normally go this…far. Something about you just got to me."

He pushed back a lock of hair that had fallen across her cheek. "I know the feeling. I was at the party to network, not find a woman who'd knock me on my ass." He cupped her jaw. "There are no rules here, Vanessa. I won't put you down for being nontraditional."

"Thanks." She squeezed his wrist. "Really. Just thanks."

He sampled a wedge of cheese and let her have a moment to recover. He also didn't want her to see how much he wanted to violently shake sense into her family. "So what happened after you caused trouble?"

"I moved out. I got a job. I went to culinary school. I got the tattoo, and my mother was humiliated and furious, but she realized I was serious about—" Her eyes popped wide. "I never saw your tattoo!"

During the heat of their connection, he'd forgotten about it. "How could you have missed it?"

One hand lying on the back of his bar stool and the other gripping his thigh, she leaned close. "Where?"

"Before, you wanted to know what."

"So where?"

He grinned. "I'm available for show and tell anytime you are."

She jiggled his thigh. "Come on, Lucas. Tell."

"I'll show instead."

He rose from his stool and unbuttoned his jeans. Loving the eagerness and desire in her eyes, he turned his back and flipped the waistband over, knowing what she'd see on the back of his left hip. He was fairly certain he'd surprised her again.

"It's a rose," she said after a moment, the excitement in her tone draining.

"Mmm."

"I was thinking it would be…"

He glanced at her over his shoulder. "What?"

"Something else."

"A dragon?"

She wrinkled her nose. "No."

"A snake."

"No way."

"Maybe an anchor?"

"Definitely not."

"You've got a problem with roses?"

"Well…no."

"You're allergic?"

"No."

She grabbed his arm and jerked him around to face her. Of course, he took the opportunity to get closer. He wedged himself between her thighs and braced his hands on her hips. The scent of his soap rose from her skin. Desire and possession surrounded him, and he breathed deeply, praying he could hold himself in check. A least for a little while longer.

"A rose?" she asked, still confused.

"I lost a bet."

She waggled her fingers in a come-on gesture. "You've got to do better than that." When he hesitated, she added, "I'll tell you my story."

"Ladies first."

"Mia and I got them on graduation night from culinary school. We'd celebrated with a little champagne." At his skeptical look, she added, "Well, *a lot* of champagne, and the next thing we knew we were at the tattoo parlor getting decorated. Mia got a chameleon on her hip, and I got the butterfly."

"Why the butterfly?"

"Because I finally felt free, and alive, for the first time."

"It suits you."

"I think so. Now, your turn."

"I don't think you'll like it."

"A deal's a deal."

"So it is. I got mine in high school. I bet another guy I could, ah…get a certain girl into bed before he did."

She angled her head. The expression in her eyes wasn't complimentary. "Men are pigs."

"Definitely. I was young, *chère*. Forgive me? I lost, after all."

"One, I can't imagine you losing. Two—" she slid her hand across his shoulder and cupped the back of his head "—I really like when you call me that."

"I'll keep doing it then." In Cajun French, he whispered a naughty suggestion in her ear. "Now you know all my secrets."

"I do?"

He smiled. "No."

"We don't know each other at all."

Leaning forward, he tongued her earlobe. "I can fix that."

She let her head fall back on a deep sigh, exposing her throat, which he took full advantage of. He laid his lips against her warm, pine-scented skin, dragging his mouth along her jaw, then down her neck, pushing his hands beneath the robe, then pushing it off her shoulders.

His heart hammered in his chest as more of her beautiful body was revealed, and his own body throbbed in response. Was she part of his path to redeem himself from past sins? Or would she be a new sin he'd be compelled to atone for?

He wished like hell he could turn off his conscience and embrace hedonism as he once had, but his inner sense of duty—from wherever it had sprung—had been given a voice, and it wasn't likely to be silenced again.

Though the sound of Vanessa's ragged, need-filled breathing could no doubt drown out any sensible thought he managed to form.

Placing slow, lingering kisses along her neck and shoulders, he untied the robe, sliding his hands up her bare sides to cup her breasts. His thumbs brushed the peaks, which hardened like pebbles.

She moaned again, her eyes still closed, while he, on the other hand, kept his wide open. Seeing the flush of desire creep over her skin was a sight he didn't intend to miss.

He continued moving his thumbs back and forth across her nipples. She moved sinuously, pushing herself more firmly into his touch. Heat surged through his body. Watching her give herself over to pleasure so shamelessly made him as hard as a rock.

How had he fallen under her spell so quickly, so completely? He wanted to breathe her in, bind her to him.

For tonight, at least, he could.

Gently, he replaced his hands with his mouth. He laved her warm, smooth skin; he teased her nipples with his tongue. When he suckled one nipple into his mouth, she cried out and gripped his shoulders.

He reveled in her softness, her beauty and openness. His body ached, while his senses soaked in every touch, moan and gasp. Their first time had been a desperate, needy firestorm. This was a sigh, a slow breeze stirring a moonlit lake, building and billowing outward as the sensations grew more intense, more powerful.

Needing to get closer to her, to absorb her warmth, he lifted her legs, hooking them around his hips, drawing her to the edge of the bar stool, fitting himself tight between the juncture of her silky thighs. She sighed his name, and he smiled, cupping the back of her head, bringing her lips against his, even as their lower bodies molded together. Throbbing. Pulsating.

Even though he still wore his jeans, he swore he could feel her wet heat. She rolled her hips, her bare flesh scraping across the fly of his jeans. He could only imagine how the rough fabric must feel against her raw nerve endings.

The idea was erotic, intoxicating. Much like everything about the lady herself. She tasted like no other woman he'd ever kissed. She was unique in a world of sameness. Unforgettable. Special.

Her sighs had him gritting his teeth. He wanted to drive himself inside her, feel her close tightly around him like a fist of silken delight.

"Oh, Lucas," she breathed.

Sensing she was close to climax, he slid his hands down her stomach, pressing his thumbs into her. He teased her with a stroke up, then down, before centering his thumbs on her clitoris.

Her hips pumped; she moaned and thrashed. She was on the edge. He nearly came himself at the sight of the pleasure and torture dancing across her flushed face.

He moved his thumb roughly over the tip of her desire. He pressed hard, relentlessly urging her to the peak.

She went over in a rush, her body bucking, flooding his hand.

Even as he relished her satisfaction, his own needs throbbed for attention. Now.

Before she caught her breath, he'd unbuttoned his jeans, slid on protection and driven himself inside her.

She jerked in surprise, her eyes still dilated from the intensity of her orgasm.

"Go up again," he said, withdrawing, then surging forward.

Her eyes fluttered closed. She gripped his biceps in her fists. She squeezed her inner muscles around his hardness.

Gritting his teeth, he held onto his control by a thread. And, like her, he was suddenly in no mood for teasing touches or butterfly kisses. Lust drove him. Need roared through his veins.

The pinnacle hovered just out of reach. He pounded himself into her. Her hips slapping against his as she, too, rode the wave of hunger they couldn't seem to sate.

The wave finally crested, and he poured himself into her as her cries mingled with his quick thrusts. *Punch, slam, boom,* his climax roared over him like an out-of-control locomotive.

Sweat pouring off him, he held her close as small pulses continued to punch through his body.

He could become addicted to her so very easily.

"Do you really want to keep me around?" she asked as she fought for breath.

"Very much."

4

VANESSA, HER MUSCLES SORE from the night of lust, crept out of bed at 4:00 a.m.

As she fumbled through a guilty hop-step into her rebel-girl dress, she couldn't help her gaze sliding to the luscious form on the rumpled bed.

He was sprawled on his stomach, the white sheet flung across his hips, his dark hair mussed from her fingers, his profile strong, but relaxed in sleep. Illuminated by the light from the bathroom, his broad, tanned back rippled with muscles. She even got a partial glimpse of his rose tattoo.

Amazing.

With a sigh of contentment—and of regret—she slipped from the bedroom. Dangling her slingbacks from two fingers, she tiptoed down the hall toward the kitchen. She'd leave Lucas a note.

Tacky?

Probably. But her etiquette coach—aka her mother—wasn't around at the moment. And she sincerely doubted the inevitable parting after screwing a guy you've known just hours five times in one night was covered in the *Proper Girls of Atlanta* manual.

She found a pad and pen in the drawer nearest the phone. *Those helpful moving folks again.* Poised to find the right words when she had no idea how she felt about what they'd done beyond unexpected, scandalous...*amazing,* she jolted when she heard his voice.

"There's just not a proper ring to 'thanks for the sex,' is there?"

She spun to face him. He stood in the hall, leaning against the wall. Again he wore only his jeans. He did have the most *amazing* body. Even better, he knew what to do with it.

"I, uh...Lucas—" She laid down the pen and self-consciously raked her fingers through her tangled hair. "I have to go."

He pushed away from the wall, his gaze locked on hers as he moved toward her. "No, you don't. But you can if you'd feel more comfortable."

"I would." She paused, biting her lip. She couldn't remember the last time she felt this off balance. "It's been great, but I need to cater tomorrow night. Ah, make that tonight. I need to get some sleep."

Once he reached her, he extended his hand, sliding his knuckles down her cheek.

She shivered. He'd explored, pounded, licked and touched more parts of her body than she'd believed she'd had erogenous zones. But she had to regroup. She had to figure out what this carnal night really meant. He'd said he wanted to keep her around. But for how long? And was that really possible? Could any kind of relationship develop from a one-night stand?

"I'm sorry I kept you up," he said softly.

"You didn't." She felt her face flush.

Good God, she was an adult. Impulsive maybe, but not idiotic. This was ridiculous. *Find your spine, girl. Thank the man, then get out.*

"Of course you did." She leaned forward, laid her palm on his bare chest and kissed him lightly. "And it was a pleasure. But I need to get home."

She brushed past him, and he followed her without comment as she scooted into the foyer.

"I'll follow you to your car," he said.

"No, really. I'm fine."

He reached into the hall closet for a pale gray fleece jacket, which he slipped into and zipped. "It's late. You're not going into the parking garage alone." Without asking if she wanted it, he helped her into a black jacket of the same soft material. As she zipped it up, he added, "It might be cool out."

They walked out, and Vanessa felt a weird pleasure and panic rise in her throat. "I'll give it back to you once I get to my car."

"Keep it."

"How will I get it back to you?"

"My business card is in the right pocket. Call me."

How'd he manage to do that without her noticing? "Okay."

"Or mail it to me. My office address is on the card, too."

Mail? Was he giving her an out or trying to distance himself?

Do you really want to keep me around?

Very much.

That didn't sound like distance. But what would happen when he found out who she was?

He wasn't with her father's firm, so would his competitive nature demand that he cozy up to her or shun her? Which would be worse?

In a city the size of Atlanta, you'd think she could find a man not connected to her family's sphere of influence. She had, of course. Bartenders, a club DJ, a chef at a local restaurant. She'd dated them, had fun sometimes, endured disasters for a few, but she'd never worried about her last name the way she had before she'd moved out of her parents' house.

Back then she'd endured awkward setups—though her sister occasionally still managed to foist one of those on her even now through "accidental" meetings with sons of her father's cronies and parties where parents worried about social standing instead of pranks and underage drinking.

Tonight, she had to fall orgasm over orgasm for a wealthy Louisiana lawyer who'd either be groaningly impressed by her pedigree or dismissive of the family's ultraconservative reputation.

Neither scenario held much hope for her and Lucas.

"I don't want this to end tonight," he said when they reached her car.

Even as her heart jumped, she opened the door. "Neither do I."

"But you're not offering your business card."

"If you really want to, you could find me."

"So this is like a test?"

She sighed. "No. I just—I'm tired. I need to think." She tilted her head and smiled. "Tonight was wonderful."

"Yes, it was."

It felt weird leaving him. She was afraid once the magic of this night ended, nothing would be the same. Their tenuous bond would be broken.

Swallowing emotions she had no chance of working her way through at the moment, she leaned toward him, intending to kiss him lightly. But he held her against him, deepening the kiss. Just as her head threatened to spin off her shoulders, he retreated.

"Sleep well, *chère.*"

Stunned and out of breath, she dropped into the driver's seat, then managed to start the car and pull away. So much of her life was just as she wanted it, then other parts were a tangled mess. She could certainly add Lucas Broussard to the chaos.

All the way back to her apartment, instead of thinking of him, she forced herself to think of the party the next night. Hell, later *today.*

What prep work needed to be done? She and Mia were catering a small business dinner at the new home of a pharmaceutical rep. His company manufactured a popular heart medication that her cardiologist brother-in-law and many others prescribed for their patients. This dinner— consisting of caviar, lobster and grilled shrimp kebabs, no less—was the rep's way of saying *Thanks for pushing our drug!*

Personally, she found the whole business shockingly close to graft, but as long as his food-service check didn't bounce...

She had to call her supplier this morning to be sure the seafood was on its way, then she had mounds of potatoes to peel for the au gratin casserole. She had champagne to chill. Toast points and all the caviar accoutrements to assemble.

Sleep's a luxury I'm not sure I can afford.

Despite what she'd told Lucas about being tired, she didn't see how she could sleep now. Her brain was wired, even if her body was weary.

When she opened the back door to the bakery—her and Mia's apartment was on the second floor of the building— she decided to shower and change quickly, get some of the prep work done, then take a nap some time in the afternoon when Mia could monitor the counter out front.

She tiptoed upstairs to shower. The hallway split her and Mia's mini apartments in half. Each side had its own bedroom, bathroom and walk-in closet and the interior space reflected its owner's sense of style. Mia's taste ran toward jewel tones like purple, jade and turquoise. Vanessa had chosen bold colors like red, yellow and black. They'd met in the hallway with purple on one side and yellow on the other.

With a smile, Vanessa remembered the day they'd given their mothers a simultaneous tour. Different as they were, the two women had been equally horrified by the color explosion. Elise Douglas preferred pastels. Tawny Medini Swaggart Josephson Pauley didn't know what she preferred. She wasn't big on commitment.

The door to Mia's room was closed, so Vanessa hoped the insulation would be enough to mask her predawn movements.

After showering, she dressed in jeans and a green T-shirt that said, Let Me Drop Everything and Work on *Your* Problem. She flipped on the lights in the bakery's workroom, then lugged a case of champagne into the walk-in fridge. She pulled eggs, chives and red onion off the shelves and dumped them on the counter; she checked the stock of ice in the freezer. Seeing they had plenty, she noticed Mia's ice sculpture was tucked in the back. It was an excellent replica of the caduceus—the physician's symbol—which would be part of the appetizer table decoration that night.

When Vanessa had suggested a replica of the eighteenth green at the Tournament Players Club at Sugarloaf Country Club would be more appropriate, Mia had roared with laughter.

Their client, however, probably wouldn't have been amused.

As she put the eggs into a pot of water and turned the stovetop on high, her mind leaped to Lucas. Had he gone back to sleep? Or was he working, too?

She pictured him staring out that huge window in his apartment, watching the night sky, wondering what the pink light of dawn would bring.

"Hell," she said aloud to the empty room. "One night, and he's turned me into a romantic."

Vanessa thought of herself as practical, not dreamy. Her bank balance forced her to be. But practical and semipoor was way better than flighty and wealthy. Just look at her sister.

Speaking of whom...she supposed she'd better brace herself for her younger sibling's not-so-gentle nudge toward the latest bachelor on the lookout for a proper wife. As ballsy as she was, even Vanessa didn't have the guts to tell her sister that when she was attracted to a guy,

her ring finger was the least of the body parts she thought
about.

Definitely too shocking for Angelica's ears.

Though at least her sister did recommend Vanessa's
bakery to her friends. Unlike their mother, who pretended
not to know Vanessa when she was "playing servant."

"What would people think?" she always asked, her
icy-blond eyebrows raised.

*That you know the best cheesecake chef in the city? Or
maybe that you're philanthropic and always notice the
little people?* Would life really stop if people thought
Elise Douglas allowed her daughter to go her own way?
To do something she loved instead of doing what was
expected?

Yes, apparently, it would.

Striving to ignore the ache in the pit of her stomach and
knowing she wasn't likely to mend the tension between
her and her mother this early in the morning, Vanessa
tackled food prep. A much more positive activity.

For the caviar toppings, she cooled the eggs once
they'd boiled, then chopped them along with the chives
and red onions. She put each condiment into separate
dishes and stored them in the fridge alongside the caviar,
sour cream and vodka. She washed, peeled and sliced
potatoes for the rich, cheesy casserole, which she assembled and put in the fridge. She'd cook it partway before
she left for the party, then finish the baking at the rep's
house, which supposedly had a brand-new Jenn-Air con-
vection oven.

Superior equipment was always a plus, since she'd
once resorted to a trip to the store for a portable hibachi

after a client had claimed his gas grill was "top of the line," only to discover that was true except that he hadn't used it in two years and had left it uncovered during that time, and the whole bottom had rusted out.

After the seafood delivery arrived, she stored the feisty lobster in the fridge, then washed, peeled and deveined the shrimp before sliding them on wooden skewers for grilling. She made wine-lemon and pesto dipping sauces. She clarified butter. She made baguettes. She made fresh batches of cinnamon rolls, coffee cakes and orange scones for the regular Saturday-morning customers who stopped by the bakery. She even made beignets—in honor of Lucas.

Clear reflections or decisions about her night with him, however, she was fresh out of. The night had been promising and terrifying. Her body was sore and rejuvenated. Her brain was confused and stimulated.

She wanted to know more about him; she feared him finding out more about her.

Her love life, she supposed, had its wild and erratic moments, but this was a damn mess.

By the time she heard footsteps echoing on the floor overhead, it was after ten. She sipped a mocha latte and waited for her roommate to appear.

Which Mia did a couple of minutes later, wearing a bright yellow halter top and snug, blue-jean capris. Her hair was tousled. Her eyes were sleepy.

And Colin Leavy shuffled along behind her.

"Well, I'll be damned," Vanessa muttered.

Mia actually blushed.

Vanessa cleared her throat. It wasn't uncommon for Mia to have overnight guests. But *Colin?*

He was ridiculously devoted to her, so Mia was naturally suspicious. Then again, after her mother's four failed marriages, Mia was suspicious of everyone.

"Sweet roll, anyone?" Vanessa asked, nodding at the batch she'd just taken out of the oven.

Colin's uneasy glance slid to Mia. "Love one. And do I smell coffee?"

"Regular?" Vanessa walked toward the swinging door that led to the front of the shop. "I can also make espresso and lattes."

Colin groaned as if he was in desperate need of caffeine.

Maybe there were a lot of sleepless people last night.

"Espresso, please," he said. "Two shots."

"I'll help," Mia said, scooting after Vanessa.

In the bakery, Mia didn't help. She leaned against the glass-fronted display case and banged her head on the top. "What have I done?"

"Had a great time?" Vanessa asked with her eyebrows raised.

"I had a *fabulous* time," Mia moaned.

"That makes two of us," Vanessa said as she packed espresso grounds. "Or is it four?"

Mia lifted her head. "You, too?" She raced over to the espresso machine. "No kidding? Oh, God. With all *my* drama last night I nearly forgot about you and the luscious lawyer. When did you get home?"

"Four."

"Jeez. Was it great? *Of course* it was great if you stayed till four. Oh, wow. Both of us, the same night. Great sex, unlikely partners. What are the odds?"

"Pretty long."

Mia's smile was mischievous. "Speaking of long…care to spill…*details?*"

The bell above the door chimed, and Mia turned to greet the customer—a man and his daughter, clamoring for a half-dozen sweet rolls.

Vanessa smiled as she watched her partner charm them. Mia—with her great sense of style—had designed the bakery in bright shades of blue, yellow and green, giving the shop a sense of cheer and prosperity. A glass case ran across the room, showcasing the baked goods. The rolls, cakes and scones Vanessa had made earlier. Doughnuts dipped in chocolate and sprinkles. Blueberry and banana-nut muffins. Five varieties of cheesecake. Fruit parfaits and pies. Mocha tortes. Brownies. Truffles. Southern specialties like divinity and pralines.

The mural that dominated one wall of the bakery had been expertly painted by a local artist Mia had dated and featured piping hot loaves of bread sliding out of the oven, chocolate cakes and glistening fruit tarts so perfect in detail you could almost smell them. In front of the mural sat a table with a display for the catering business—menus, sample gift bags and a drawing for a free-for-twenty party that they gave away each July and December.

When the customers left, Mia grinned at Vanessa. "So the *long* details?"

"I didn't pull out a ruler." She paused as the espresso spurted into the cup. "Still, everything was…healthy. And he has magical hands."

"I never imagined Colin was so *inventive.* We did it all over the place—the floor, the bed, the counter."

"The *shop* counter?" Vanessa asked, glancing around.

"Hey, I used the antibacterial wipes afterward."

Mia giggled, and Vanessa joined her. They hugged liked giddy drunks. Lack of sleep and great sex undoubtedly contributed to their buoyant moods.

Mia dabbed tears from her eyes as Vanessa started steaming the milk. "I'm punchy. But I did talk to Peter's manager, who scored you two tickets to his client's performance in a couple of weeks."

Peter was an old friend who'd single-handedly started a resurgence of Rat Pack–era music with a tribute band. The tickets were traded like gold. "You're a gem."

"I'm exhausted, and we've still got to start on that food prep for Rex Johnson's party."

"Mmm. Well, you'll be pleased to hear I felt a bit energetic this morning and already started on it."

"Excellent. I've still got to do the party bags."

The party bags—something that used to be found only at kids' birthday parties—had become an adult party staple.

As with everything, blame it on Hollywood. From the Oscar presenters to CD launch parties, guests in the entertainment industry were treated to portable DVD players, sunglasses, luxury cosmetics and spa trips. Since most people—especially well-off people—wanted to feel like stars in their own lives, the trend had trickled down to the nonfamous crowd.

The addition of bags was a great source of additional income to Dessert First, since Mia was a whiz at putting together luscious, expensive-looking goodies, many times filled with items donated by local businesses for targeted advertising.

For tonight's soiree, Mia had gotten massage and facial coupons, skin-care samples, custom CDs of the music their client planned to play during the party, scented candles, cookies from the bakery, colorful candies in the shape of syringes and stethoscopes, plus some pens, magnets and prescription pads printed with the pharmaceutical logos.

"What are you going to do about Colin?" Vanessa asked, veering off work for the personal stuff that had so dominated her thoughts the last few hours.

Mia shrugged. "Go with it. For the moment, anyway. What about you?"

"I have no idea." Her friend's boldness was inspiring, though. "Partywise, I'll help with the bags. We'll finish the prep, then take turns stuffing the bakery and napping."

Mia toasted her with her foamy latte. "Partners."

"Forever."

"I CAN'T LET YOU DO THIS."

Joseph Douglas folded his hands on his desk and studied the woman across from him.

Millicent Switzer's normally clear, laughing blue eyes were clouded and bloodshot. Her platinum hair had lost some of its lovely sheen.

He'd loved her once. Some part of him always would, he supposed. She might have been his wife, the mother of his children, if he'd followed his heart instead of his head.

But, of course, he hadn't. He'd dated and proposed to Elise instead.

She'll be so perfect to lead the foundation, his mother had insisted. *Her family is like ours,* his father had added.

Millicent, on the other hand, had been interested in a career of her own—fashion design—not running the Douglas Foundation. Her family wasn't like his—that is, they didn't have money. Old money, anyway.

He'd bowed to his parents' pressure, and she'd eventually married Gilbert Switzer, who'd had plenty of old money and who'd eventually convinced Millicent to give up her career. She'd made a wonderful volunteer director of the Burton Wing of the fine arts museum.

He didn't appreciate the irony.

Still, he didn't regret his decision all those years ago. He'd eventually grown to love Elise, made himself a respected home of his own and carried on the Douglas tradition of law and philanthropy.

"You're a good friend," Millie went on. "I appreciate you thinking of me." She shook her head, her limp fall of hair brushing the tops of her shoulders. "But you can't."

Joseph smiled slightly. "It's done."

"You'll be disbarred, arrested."

"No, I won't."

"I'll be fine. I can go back to work. I never should have given up my design dreams anyway."

"You're getting the money, Millie. I won't hear another argument about it."

"What if—" She bit her lip. "What if *she* says something?"

"It won't matter. She won't be believed. She's a stripper for God's sake."

Less than two weeks ago, Millie's respected neurosurgeon husband had dropped dead in the bed of a stripper in Daytona Beach. Though the family had managed to keep most of the humiliating details out of the papers, rumors were still flying, laughter still gurgled beneath the surface of condolences.

Also unfortunately for Millie and her three sons, a month before his death, Gilbert had changed his will, cutting his wife out of his thirty-million-dollar estate and including Candy, the pink-haired stripper. The lunatic had even made Candy executor of his sons' trust funds.

When Gilbert had come to his office to record this ridiculous document, Joseph had laughed in his face. He'd refused to file the will with the state, assuring Gilbert that he'd quickly change his mind.

But Gilbert had insisted on the change, and he'd threatened to go to another attorney. So Joseph had done something he never had—at least to a client. He'd lied.

He'd told Gilbert he'd filed the new will, though he had no intention of ever doing so. The old will would stand, and his friend would thank him when he changed his mind.

The law was supposed to be blind. The people entrusted to dispense and defend it fiercely loyal. Joseph knew he wasn't allowed to judge his clients. He was obligated to be their instrument within the law. He'd done so without fail for almost thirty years.

But he couldn't file that document. He couldn't leave a loyal wife and mother with nothing, just because she'd signed a prenuptial agreement, and reward some silicone-enhanced bubblehead, who'd obviously given Gilbert some kind of drug to get him to change his will.

What an idiot. No decent man would bring such humiliation on his family. If his client hadn't already died, Joseph would have strangled him personally. But he was dead, and no one, save him, Millie and his law clerk, would ever know about the other will.

And maybe a Daytona Beach stripper.

He cast a quick glance around his pristine office. The oxblood-colored leather furniture, the calm landscape paintings, the solid mahogany desk and cabinets, the books, awards and objets d' art. He'd both inherited and earned them. His experience with the law gave him a perspective that escaped most men. He deserved to right a few more wrongs.

Millie's eyes filled with tears. "He said he was leaving me. He was going to marry her."

"He didn't." *Thank God.* Then Joseph really would have had a mess on his hands. "How are the boys holding up?" he asked in an effort to shift the subject.

Millie clenched her hands in her lap. She glanced nervously around his office. "They're…embarrassed. The kids at school have obviously heard the…rumors. The…circumstances. Of course half the teasing comes with a pleaded introduction to *that woman.*"

Millie had two sons at Georgia Tech and another who had established a thriving family practice in the suburbs. How Joseph would have liked one of his girls to see the doctor's appeal. Of course Angelica had married well, and Vanessa… Well, there was no telling that child anything.

"The scandal will pass," he said to Millie. "Brian has been a wonderful family spokesman. You've done such a great job—"

"Are all men led around by their dicks?" she bit out, jumping to her feet.

Joseph flinched at her tone and crude language. Millie

was the epitome of a proper, elegant Southern lady, though he supposed she had a right to her anger.

"No, Millie," he said, rising and moving around the desk toward her. "They're not. Something happened to Gilbert. She drugged him—"

She barked out a laugh. "Right."

"—or he was going through some kind of crisis." He grasped her hands in his. "He would have come to his senses. I'm sure of it. He would have come back on his knees, begging you to forgive him, grateful to have such a beautiful wife."

She glanced down at their joined hands, then back up at him. "I don't know what I'd do without you, Joseph."

He could smell her expensive perfume. He fought against unwanted desire. "You're strong, Millie. You're going to survive this."

She took a deep breath, then turned away. "I guess." She walked across his office and gazed out the floor-to-ceiling windows. Beyond her, he could see the Atlanta skyline. An expanse of gray-blue sky set against a collection of vertical steel columns. He knew if he looked down he'd see the familiar hustle and bustle of the city. The whole business made him tired.

Maybe he really was getting old.

"I almost hired a gigolo last night," Millie said quietly.

"You *what?*"

She turned to look at him over her shoulder. A smile hovered at her lips. "A gigolo. A man you pay to have sex with you."

"Good God, Millie. What are you thinking? Now's not the time—"

"To let my libido do the thinking? You're wrong, Joseph, now's the *perfect* time."

The sexual tension in the room was palpable. Joseph had been tempted before—what man could say he hadn't?—but he'd never betrayed his wife. A man had a duty to his family, an obligation to loyalty. Despite the strayings of his clients and contemporaries, he had no intention of bringing down scandal on his family or disrespect on himself and his firm.

He had to regain control of this meeting. "I know this has been a nightmare for you, but revenge isn't the answer. You'll regret it later."

"I don't see how."

Great. How would that look? If the stripper did challenge the will, he certainly didn't need the grieving widow holed up in a local hotel with some hired lothario.

"Just go about your normal routine. Wait until we get this will through probate."

"Okay." She sniffed, then flung herself into his arms. "Oh, Joseph, what am I going to do? I'm so miserable!"

With that, his wife walked into his office.

5

LUCAS SWIVELED HIS home-office chair to face the window behind his desk. Towering steel buildings dotted the skyline. Heavy, charcoal clouds hovered behind them. Rain would undoubtedly ruin trips to the lake and pool in the afternoon. Afterward, the humidity wouldn't decrease. It would just produce steam. Summertime in the South.

He had projects to work on—a pro bono case he was pursuing for a widow, calls to make regarding the law student he was mentoring—but he didn't move.

Where is she now?

In his mind, he watched her turn, glance at him over her shoulder and smile. He smiled in return. He walked slowly toward her; he stroked her cheek, pushing her hair back behind her ear....

Though he knew obsessing about Vanessa was a bad idea, he indulged himself anyway. He recalled her enthusiasm for her business, her playful indulgence with the party guests, her rapturous expressions as they made love.

Pick up the phone.

No.

He couldn't logically explain his sudden reluctance to find out who she was. But he trusted his instincts. The fantasy, the mystery of last night still hovered in the air like rolling fog. He didn't want the clouds to clear.

Ridiculous.

Resolving to get to Vanessa later, he shook off the ghosts of trepidation and turned to his computer. With the odd encounter at the party last night between him and "Anthony," the drunk junior executive from Douglas and Alderman, foremost in his mind, he searched Google for the attorneys, starting with Douglas.

What was going on with the ultraconservative firm? Generations of moldy money and community respect *could* produce scandal, but it was generally quiet. An embezzling charge or two, infidelity occasionally, a trust fund purged for drugs once in a while. Unfortunately, it happened in every community.

From Douglas and Alderman, however, he hadn't heard a whisper of negative gossip. They appeared to staunchly support their clients, discreetly defended them in court when necessary—which was hardly ever—and quietly cashed the checks of the privileged as reward for a job well done.

He couldn't imagine what had convinced a junior partner to babble on about something amiss at the firm that was his livelihood.

It had to be something big. *Ya can't have two wills. Ya just can't.* Two wills—at least for one person—was definitely not a good thing. For a lawyer or a beneficiary.

In the computer search, unsurprisingly, the Douglas Foundation came up first. It, after all, was the only Douglas enterprise that actually *wanted* publicity. Of only the respectable kind.

He skimmed through a couple of articles about monetary recipients from the foundation—the United Way, the Cancer Society, the children's hospital among them. All were respectable and expected. He glanced at a few posed publicity photographs lifted from newspapers, featuring the foundation's director, Elise Douglas, who looked vaguely familiar.

He moved on to sites specifically mentioning the firm of Douglas and Alderman. There wasn't much. Their primary objective was, after all, discretion. A lawsuit won here and there that had minor public interest. A client caught in an affair-with-the-secretary scandal, where the firm tried—unsuccessfully—to get their guy custody of his two children.

The firm didn't even have a Web site.

Next, he checked on the other name Anthony had mentioned—Switzer. He found some articles there. Gilbert Switzer was a prominent neurosurgeon, who'd been praised for both his medical skills and generosity, giving often to the art museum. He and his wife, Millicent, were high-society pillars, obviously moving in the same elite circles as the Douglases. There was even a picture of the four of them together at the opening of the new cardiac wing of a downtown hospital.

But Gilbert Switzer had died last month of a massive heart attack at age fifty-eight.

"Kind of young," Lucas muttered as he gazed at the screen.

The article on his death was long on accomplishments, but short on details about what had led up to his death.

Mr. Switzer, away from Atlanta on a business trip to

Florida, was pronounced dead at Halifax Medical Center in Daytona Beach.

So Switzer had died in Daytona Beach, where Anthony had said the stripper lived. *Interesting.* A connection and a fact verified. But there were no details about the manner of his death.

Frustrated, but still intrigued, Lucas went back to the Douglas search, looking for anything mentioning *Anthony* or any vague reference to the personal life of Joseph. Next to nothing. A mention of a Businessman of the Month award. A few pictures at society functions.

Lucas called a colleague at the American Bar Association and left a message for him to call Monday. Maybe there were complaints at the bar involving Anthony or Joseph Douglas.

Back to the Internet, Lucas scrolled through the society photos. Pictures of Douglas and his wife at something called the Peach State Bowl, then him and his whole family at last year's Douglas Foundation Christmas party.

A beautiful blonde smiled back at him. His heart jumped as he read the caption.

Pictured with Joseph Douglas are his wife, Elise, and his two daughters, Angelica and Vanessa.

"YOU GIRLS HAVE DONE a beautiful job," Rex Johnson said, raising his wineglass in a toast. "As always."

Vanessa was fairly certain she hadn't been a *girl* since age seventeen, but she smiled benignly at her client anyway. "Thanks so much, Rex."

Mia—serving from the other side of the table—rolled

her eyes. "We live to feed people," she said, demonstrating what a good sport she was.

They ought to get an award for sportsmanship. One guest had shown up drunk, then tried to make a sloppy pass at the chief of cardiology's wife. Hoping to dilute some of the alcohol, Mia had stuffed him full of French bread in the kitchen during the appetizer course. Meanwhile, their host spent so much time patting himself on the back for doing nothing more than making the phone call to hire them that Vanessa was sure he'd have bruises.

The conversation that flowed among the men was boring and self-promoting. The only thing the women seemed to be concerned about was the latest designer handbag. At least Vanessa's sister had thrown an encouraging smile her way every once in a while.

"How's your transplant patient, Dr. Orley?" her sister asked as she forked up a bite of shrimp.

Dr. Orley—whose young, pretty third wife had been the object of the earlier pass—swirled lobster in butter sauce. "Very well. A challenging case, as I'm sure you've heard…"

Vanessa tuned out their conversation as she strode into the kitchen. She started brewing the coffee just as Mia walked in.

"Girls?" her friend asked, her hands planted on her hips.

"It's a feminist thing most people don't realize bothers anybody."

"Humph."

"It doesn't help that our patience has waned."

Mia sank against the counter, her sassy bun drooping a bit. "Last night is catching up with us."

Vanessa stifled a yawn and glanced at her watch. "We should be out of here in less than three hours, then we can collapse."

"How did you leave things with Lucas this morning?"

"Vaguely open. He gave me his business card." And a fleece jacket that she'd found herself holding to her face several times during the day, just to breathe in his scent.

Mia wrinkled her nose. "Business card? Not very romantic."

But it suited her. How Lucas had known it would, she had no idea. "You and Colin seemed pretty cozy when he left."

"We're going boating on Lake Lanier tomorrow."

"You in a bikini alone with Colin?" Vanessa eyed her friend's petite but curvy frame. "He might want to consider hiring a driver. He'll wreck the boat staring at you."

"He's seen all there is to see already."

"I'd still keep a life jacket handy."

"You could invite Lucas to come with us and supervise."

"I doubt that's what Colin has in mind."

"Are you going to see him again?"

"Colin? Well, our taxes are already done, so—"

"I mean Lucas, goofy."

Vanessa retrieved stacks of coffee cups and plates from the cabinet overhead. "Maybe."

"Do you want to?"

Yes! But she bit her lip before quietly saying, "I think so."

Mia tossed up her hands. "Oh, good grief, Vanessa.

What's with you today? You don't have to marry the man. Just ask him to dinner."

For all her rebelliousness against her proper family, Vanessa couldn't escape the idea that she'd done something bad. Something wild, reckless and impulsive that— yet again—would lead to trouble. But how could something that felt so good be wrong? On the other hand, didn't rebellion always feel good in the beginning?

"Dinner?" How did she explain her feelings seemed too heavy to resort to polite dinner conversation? They'd skipped over several getting-to-know-you, dating and foreplay steps last night. Did they now have to go backward to go forward? When he moved his hand she would recall how his touch felt against her skin, the intense pleasure he could create. When he smiled, she'd remember the taste of him on her lips.

Mia leaned forward, staring into her eyes. "I suggest you do it quick—before you spontaneously combust."

Vanessa rolled her shoulders. "I have no idea what you're talking about."

"You weren't just thinking about hot sex with him?"

"Well…"

"I'd say you've got a little more passion to burn through."

"Is that what you're doing with Colin? Burning through your passion?"

"You bet your ass."

"I should call him." Though that would again make her the pursuer, not pursuee.

Mia snagged the coffeepot. "Yes, you should."

This indecision wasn't like her. She hadn't questioned

her instincts in a long time. Was Lucas the cause, or was this quest to reunite with her family responsible?

Both ideas were troubling.

She and Mia returned to the dining room just in time to hear Angelica say, "Speaking of lawsuits...have you all heard that the ambulance-chasing Lucas Broussard has moved into our city?"

Vanessa nearly dropped her tray. Lucas wasn't— He couldn't be—

She exchanged an anxious look with Mia as her brother-in-law added, "He even showed up at the fund-raiser last night."

"He's known as a cold one," someone else said.

"And the best case-win record in the history of Louisiana law."

Hands shaking, Vanessa set a cup and saucer next to her sister, who glanced up casually, as if she had no idea Vanessa's heart was beating like a jackhammer. "No coffee for me, thanks."

Vanessa nodded mutely and moved the cup to the person next to her.

"I heard he signed on with Geegan, Duluth and Patterson," one of the guests added. "He's supposed to be helping them defend against frivolous lawsuits."

"A leopard doesn't change his spots," Dr. Orley put in, as if he knew jungle cats as well as human hearts.

"Well, *I* wouldn't be surprised if he came after *us* next," Orley's buxom wife said in an I'm-snooty-and-proud-of-it voice.

"How do you—" Vanessa began, her voice trembling with anger, until Mia intruded.

"How did everyone like the lobster?" she said cheerfully. "Just yummy, don't you agree?"

Several people nodded, and Vanessa managed to swallow her feelings as she finished distributing the cups. A brief comment from her parents the week before suddenly took on new meaning.

"I can't believe *he's* coming," her mother had said.

"You did invite him," her father had commented from behind his newspaper.

"I invited the firm, not that immoral ruffian."

Lucas. She'd been talking about Lucas, Vanessa now realized. The one time she actually should have been paying attention to her mother's complaining rants, and she'd been too busy planning the fund-raiser's menu to listen.

The guests' compliments on the food died away, and her new lover again became the focus.

"I heard he once got a twenty-million-dollar judgment against a group of doctors and a hospital in New Orleans."

"Where did he go to law school?" someone asked haughtily. "Certainly not Ivy League."

"Supposedly his father's in jail."

"Why did he come here?"

"Do you really think he stakes out the emergency room?"

Vanessa couldn't listen to any more and rushed into the kitchen, the silver serving tray still miraculously clutched in her bloodless hands.

As she set it on the counter, the accusations and speculations spun through her head all over again. It wasn't possible. Lucas wasn't the man they described.

But his vagueness about his past had doubt intruding. *I practiced in New Orleans, but I'm not from there.* So where was he from? And why hadn't she pressed him for details? Why hadn't she asked more questions?

Mia burst into the kitchen just as shame and regret were taking hold of Vanessa. "Don't listen to those assholes for a second." She grabbed Vanessa's arm and spun her around. "They're exaggerating. Or going by rumor. Or downright lying out of jealousy."

"Ambulance chaser?" Vanessa whispered, horrified and embarrassed she still had enough Douglas upbringing in her to be so judgmental. Had his beautiful apartment been bought with other people's pain and suffering?

Mia squeezed her arm. "Don't do this to yourself. We'll get through dessert, then you'll call him. Talk it out."

"This is why I stay away from guys who move with this crowd."

"I know." Mia stroked her back. "Oh, honey, I know. But you can't let them make you doubt your instincts. *You* know him."

Vanessa shook her head. "I don't."

"Stop it. Think about what they said—everything from *certainly not Ivy League* to *the best case-win record in Louisiana.* The truth could be anywhere in between, or nowhere close at all."

Some of Mia's urgency finally broke thought. "Someone said he was cold. He's *not* cold."

Mia looked relieved. "Exactly."

"How dare they spread rumors and talk about him like he wasn't fit for their company?"

"Because they're jerks."

Though her stomach still trembled, Vanessa sighed. "Yes, they are."

"Let's serve dessert."

"And get the hell out of here."

Of course that plan was way too hopeful and simple. Vanessa did manage to help serve the double-chocolate cheesecake and stuff her personal problems, but as she was carrying dirty dishes back to the kitchen, her sister followed her.

"I need to talk to you," Angelica said, her face pinched with worry.

Did she know? How could she have found out *already*? Would Vanessa be forced to choose between Lucas and the possibility of peace with her family? She ached to defend Lucas, but she didn't want to completely alienate her family.

"Angelica, I really don't—"

"Mother is driving me crazy."

Vanessa stared at her. "She is?"

Her sister collapsed onto a kitchen chair. "She calls me into her office every afternoon—at precisely four-thirty—and goes through everything I've done wrong that day. She critiques my clothes, my conversations, my correspondence, even my e-mails. It's driving me crazy. I'm jumpy and snappy, which only makes my correspondence and conversations go downhill." She rolled her eyes as she paused. "Listen to me. I swear I'm turning into a parrot. Correspondence and conversations. Who talks like that anymore? Phone calls and e-mails. Just *once* I'd like to correct *her!*"

Breathing hard at the end of this tirade, her eyes filled

and her lower lip trembled. Since Vanessa recognized the signs of regret after rebellion, she pulled her sister into her arms while she cried.

"What's going—"

Vanessa waved her brother-in-law out of the kitchen. She glared when he didn't move.

Finally, he backed out.

A combination of kinship and guilt flooded Vanessa as she held her baby sister. In many ways, her leaving had doubled the pressure for Angelica. Not that she was solely responsible for her sister's choices, but the responsibilities and demands Vanessa had run from, Angelica had had to shoulder.

But Vanessa had assumed her sister relished her parents' undivided attention. She'd seemed eager to step into Vanessa's role. She was as natural as a dignified debutante.

She just needed to do things her way, not their Mother's.

Maybe Vanessa and Angelica's mutual need to make their own way would strengthen their relationship. Other than Angelica's matchmaking, Vanessa and her sister rarely shared meaningful conversations. They didn't share the same taste in clothes, shoes, makeup or hairstyles. They couldn't eat together peacefully, since Angelica was always on a strict diet. They didn't exercise together—Angelica liked yoga; Vanessa liked kickboxing. They didn't like the same books—self-help nonfiction versus romance, erotica and thrillers.

"Why don't you—"

"I shouldn't have bothered you with this," Angelica said suddenly, stepping back.

"It's fine. I'm glad you came to me."

Angelica snatched a napkin off the counter and patted her eyes. "No, I shouldn't have bothered you. I'll be fine."

"Angel, I'm always here for—"

She shook her head and backed away. Her face was red with embarrassment. "Please don't mention this to anybody."

"I wouldn't do that."

Her sister said nothing, just rushed from the room.

Then again, maybe understanding was further away than she thought.

"They're all leaving," Mia said as she bustled into the kitchen a few moments later, her arms laden with more dirty dishes. "Let's finish up and blow out of this lame-o joint."

"You're on, girl."

By the time they'd pocketed Rex's tip and loaded their van an hour later, Vanessa was drained physically and emotionally. She wanted to talk to Lucas. She wanted to avoid him. She wanted to sleep. She didn't see how she'd ever close her eyes.

As she slipped from the van at the bakery's rear door, however, the decision was ripped from her hands when Lucas emerged from a sleek, black Mercedes.

He'd found her.

He was dressed in black pants and an oatmeal-colored shirt. His dark hair was swept off his striking face. He moved with lithe grace, his shoulders wide, his waist narrow, his legs long.

Her heart, quite simply, fluttered.

"You ladies look like you could use some help," he said as he approached.

Was she happy he'd been so persistent, or apprehensive about facing him with the truth, about facing real life and not just the fantasy they'd enjoyed?

When Vanessa stared mutely at him—call it stunned lust—Mia said, "Thank God for men. Are those biceps as strong as they look?"

Lucas grinned, and all the breath left Vanessa's body. Okay, there was definitely no talking now. She remembered him carrying her to his bedroom. She recalled him bracing his body on his forearms as he hovered above her, moving in and out of her with exquisite, torturous pleasure.

"I think I can manage whatever you give me," he said, sending Vanessa a quick, heated glance.

They loaded up their arms with boxes and soon had the van unloaded and the supplies stored in the bakery's back room.

It was ten-thirty, and Vanessa had known Lucas for twenty-four hours—long enough to realize she knew next-to-nothing about him. Yet somehow she suspected that wouldn't stop her from jumping him again if given half the chance.

IN AN EFFORT TO KEEP his hands off Vanessa, Lucas wrapped them around his coffee mug. "Where were you catering tonight?"

She moved things around on the counter. Nervously, he thought. "A party for a pharmaceutical rep."

"It was a rousing success, as always," Mia said as she settled on the stool next to him at the long island that dominated the center of the room. "Lobster and shrimp. And

Vanessa made these fantastic basil-and-crabmeat-topped cucumber appetizers. Yum."

Though he'd like to talk to Vanessa alone, he was somewhat grateful for her talkative roommate at the moment. Vanessa's eyes were unfocused, her hands shaky. Regret and worry dominated her expression.

Something was up.

"Where did you two meet?" he asked, hoping to put Vanessa at ease.

"Culinary school," Mia said. "She was brilliant. I was a disaster."

"You were not," Vanessa said, turning to face them.

"I was." Mia grinned proudly. "But I have other talents."

Lucas smiled over the rim of his mug. The two women made an intriguing pair. He'd seen a bold, confident side of Vanessa the night before. Tonight, he was seeing a more serious, reflective side. He could imagine fiery Mia helping her keep perspective with both extremes.

"Care to share?" he asked.

Mia laughed and patted his arm. "You, my good man, are what us Southern ladies used to call a rogue."

"I think that's a compliment."

"It most definitely is." Mia cast a glance at Vanessa. "I can see why you fell so quickly for this one."

Vanessa's mug hit the island with a thud. "Gosh, Mia, you must be exhausted. Why don't you go on to bed? I'll finish up here."

"But I—"

Vanessa grabbed her friend's arm and tugged her away. "Can I talk to you privately for a moment?"

A short, somewhat heated discussion in the corner followed. Lucas kept his face impassive, though he was pretty certain he was the topic of conversation. While Vanessa was wary of him, Mia seemed to be solidly on his side. He wondered if it would be appropriate to send her flowers.

When the women came back, Mia was in the middle of a fake yawn. "Sorry to poop out on you guys, but I'm exhausted." She crossed to the sink and dropped off her mug before she headed toward the door. There, she cast an impish wink over her shoulder. "Be good, you two. Or better yet...don't be." With a waggle of her fingers and a wiggle of her hips, she was gone.

"Cute friend you've got," he said casually when Vanessa continued to glare mutely at the door.

"Way too cute."

"But she left us alone, which figures nicely into my plans." He patted the stool next to him. "Have a seat, Ms. Douglas, and tell me about your day."

Surprise overcame the exhaustion in her eyes. "You know who I am then? Who my family is?"

"Yes."

"And?"

He shrugged, though he felt everything *but* nonchalant about her lineage. Apprehensive, off balance, troubled and even inferior—something he'd sworn he'd never feel again. He was trying to change his life, to be a person worthy of the gifts and fortune he'd been given. He was working for others and not himself for the first time. It felt good. And right.

But he wasn't sure it was enough.

"I need to know who you are," she said.

"I imagine you do. But not tonight." The possibility of her rejection loomed. He didn't want to take that chance. Not now. Not yet. He tapped the stool again. "Sit before you fall."

To his surprise, she did. He didn't want to consider the implications of her family connections. They would be rivals in the best of circumstances. But given the information he had regarding "two wills," the distance between them was much more vast.

He'd known from the first moment he'd seen her that she came from money. Now he had to reconcile himself with *whose* money it was.

Joseph freakin' Douglas. It wasn't possible that a woman as lovely and free-spirited as Vanessa had sprung from his genes. Lucas wanted her no matter who her parents were, but it certainly made his task more difficult.

"Tonight, I want you to tell me about your day," he repeated.

To his surprise, she did. She told him about the prep, the gift bags, about Mia and some guy named Colin hooking up, about Rex Johnson and him showing off for his cardiologist guests.

"Everything was going great until…"

Not yet. He'd never apologized to anyone for his choices. He certainly didn't intend to start now. Did he?

Ridiculously, he tried to postpone the conflict he knew was coming. "You realized one of the guests was drunk?"

"We realized that when he walked in the door."

"One of the guests made a pass at another guy's wife."

"Handled that, too."

"Somebody got sick."

"Not from my food, honey."

"Somebody refused to eat."

"Actually…your name came up."

He widened his eyes. "At a dinner party of Atlanta cardiologists? Imagine that."

She jumped to her feet, and he applauded her renewed strength. Nervousness didn't suit her. "We're not going to talk about this tomorrow, because there isn't going to be a tomorrow for us until you answer a few questions."

He fell back on an old defensive mechanism he'd used many times to cover up his pain and anxiousness—flippancy. "I'd be delighted to."

She paced. "Don't get cute with me, buddy. I'm starting with a tough one."

"Please do."

"Are you an ambulance chaser?"

"You mean have I ever engaged in high-speed pursuit of an emergency-services vehicle?"

She stopped and glared at him.

"Maybe not. I'm a lawyer, darling. I do tend to take everything literally." When she said nothing, he realized his light answers, while protecting himself, were making her angry. He sobered his tone. "No, I'm not—nor have I ever been—an ambulance chaser. I got my clients through referrals."

"But you're a personal-injury attorney."

"At one time, I did practice with that specialty."

"Do you have the best case-win record in Louisiana?"

"How flattering." Her deepening scowl wasn't a comfort, however. "I have no idea if that's true, I'm afraid."

"Have you ever taken out an ad on the back of the Yellow Pages?"

"Ah...no."

"Are you and my father rivals?"

"We work for firms that have undoubtedly been on opposite sides."

"But have you personally ever faced him in court?"

"No. Your father hasn't been in a courtroom for nearly ten years, Vanessa."

"How do you know that?"

She was right. The questions were tough. "I keep track of the industry. I researched Atlanta specifically when I knew I was coming here. Your father is a big influence in this city. I know *of* him. I've never met him." And maybe his never-met opinion of the man as a pompous ass was off base. But Lucas doubted it.

"How did you find out who I was?" She paused. "And when?"

Here's where vowing to tell the truth got sticky. "I was doing some research on your father—related to a professional matter. I found a picture of him with you and your sister." He glanced at his watch. "About three hours ago. I made some calls, found out about your bakery and came over."

"Were you surprised about my background?"

"No."

She raised her eyebrows. "Really?"

"You're a classy woman, Vanessa. It shows, no matter that your job is one some people would consider less than ideal."

She nodded. "Is your father in prison?"

By damn if that didn't catch him off guard. And it

shouldn't have. "No, he's dead. I told you that last night. I didn't lie."

"I'm sorry." She turned away. "This is all none of my business."

"It is if you want it to be. The answers just may not be what you expect." He rose, laying his hands on her shoulders. He was cheered when she didn't pull away. "You need to know if the man you met last night is real or not, and it doesn't help that I'm not the most forthcoming person around. I'm not used to confiding in anybody."

She glanced back at him. "No argument there. I still don't feel like I know much more than I did."

"Then we'll have to get together and exchange life stories. How's dinner tomorrow night?"

"I...tomorrow's Saturday. I have a bachelorette party to cater."

"Then lunch. I usually work until noon. Why don't you come by the office?"

"Fine." She narrowed her eyes. "You were prepared for these questions."

"Yes, I was."

"How? How did you know I'd found out? Did someone at the party tip—"

"No!" He thrust his hand through his hair. "Like those people would ever lower themselves to talk to me." He drew a deep breath, trying to find control again. "No one at the party tipped me, though I could probably give you the guest list. I can also imagine the derision in their voices when they talked about me. I've heard it all—including all the rumors and speculation—many times over. Hell, some of them I've encouraged.

"I knew you'd heard just by looking at your face. The suspicion in your eyes was the only *tip* I needed."

Her face paled. "Lucas, I didn't mean to—" She stopped and sighed. "This whole thing is way out of my orbit. I'm crazy about you, but I don't know you. I never meant to hurt you."

In two steps, he had her in his arms. He didn't want to admit, even to himself, how much he needed her warmth and her touch.

"We'll figure it out. I'll find a way."

Hadn't he accomplished everything he'd set his mind to? Hadn't he battled odds longer than most people even dreamed? But he'd attained those dreams with ruthlessness and a careless attitude toward the means.

He'd only just begun the journey to redemption. He needed more time, more proof of his intentions, before meeting a woman like Vanessa. Would his flaws and mistakes deny him this new and precious relationship? Something he'd never had before but never realized he was missing until he'd looked into her eyes.

Leaning back, he kissed her forehead. "I need to get going."

Surprise and disappointment flickered across her face.

He didn't want to leave either, but he needed time to figure out how to tell her the things that might drive her away.

6

STUNNED, VANESSA FOLLOWED HIM to the door. "You're leaving?"

"You're exhausted, and I've thrown a lot at you." Still holding her hand, he leaned forward and kissed her cheek. Heat sizzled in his wake. "I'll see you tomorrow. About noon?"

"Sure, but—"

He smiled. Distant. Calm. "But what?"

"After last night, I thought you'd want to…"

"Screw you blind?"

How did he always manage to surprise her, knock her off balance? She blinked up at him.

He pushed her against the door. Not with violence, but with force. And command. "Oh, I do, *chère*." He pressed his rock-hard erection against her hips to prove his point. "Very much."

The bubble of confident recklessness that had served her so well over the past several years burst. Being this close to him again reminded her of the addictive heat they created together. Ever since the moment they'd parted, she'd been confused, but now she knew just what she wanted. "Prove it," she said, lifting her chin.

He stared at her for a moment, his green eyes glittering. Then his mouth captured hers.

As he thrust his tongue past her lips, she braced her hands against his chest. His heart hammered beneath her palms, even as her own pulse skipped a beat.

When fire exploded inside her, she forgot about who he was, who she was and why being together was never going to work. She had no reason to trust him, but she did. She craved his touch as much as she craved to understand why he, of all people, fascinated her.

Hunger and need flowed through her veins as easily as her blood. The urgency she felt inside was matched by his arousal. His hands cupped her butt, pressing her tighter against the hardness between his legs. Her knees went weak at the prospect of pleasure, of possessing him again.

Her nipples tightened and tingled. Warmth flowed between her legs. Just as she started to reach for the zipper on his pants to end this delicious torture, he stepped back.

Breathing hard, he stared at her. "I need to go."

"You *what?*"

"You need time and space to consider me. To consider us." He rolled his shoulders, making an obvious effort to gather himself. "Until tomorrow, *chère?*"

"Yeah. Sure." Aroused and frustrated and seeing her best chance of satisfaction opening the door, anger seemed like the best comeback. "What did you even come to see me for? What are you doing here?"

He glanced back at her, his eyes bleak and sardonic. "Atoning."

He was gone before she recovered enough to ask any more questions.

JOSEPH DOUGLAS PUSHED BACK from the table and nodded at his housekeeper. "Excellent dinner, Alice."

Alice inclined her head and cleared his plate.

"I'm going to work in the office for a while, Elise," he said to his wife as he walked from the room.

"Do you mind if I join you for a few moments?" she asked, following him. "I need to show you some financial figures for the foundation."

"Sure." It had been a long damn day, though. What he really wanted to do was pour a scotch, read the newspaper, then go over a few case files. Alone.

As he pulled the door closed behind Elise, she said, "I'd love a drink."

"I'll have Alice bring you some wine."

She laid her hand on his arm. "I'll have scotch. You do have some in here, don't you?"

Elise *never* drank liquor. He struggled to hide his surprise. "I do." He retrieved the bottle and two heavy tumblers, added ice, then poured them each a healthy measure before sitting in his chair. His wife sat on the other side of the desk. "I hope the financial state of the foundation isn't what's driven you to whiskey."

"Everything's fine there. Well, except that Angelica jumps every time the phone rings. If only she had a little of Vanessa's backbone." She sighed. "And Vanessa had her decorum." She waved her hand vaguely, then sipped from her glass. Immediately, she began to choke.

Joseph raced around the desk to pat her on the back.

"I'm...okay," she gasped, pounding her chest with her fist.

He returned to his seat, feeling his eye begin to twitch.

He'd never been a star in the courtroom, but he was an excellent analyst of the behavior and physical cues of others. He'd made the firm another fortune by launching his jury examiner panels.

"God, that never gets any better, does it?"

"That's forty-year-old scotch," he said, indignant. "And when have you ever had it?"

"I snuck some out of my parents' liquor cabinet once."

He nearly choked on his own sip. "You did?"

"Once." She tossed back the rest of the liquor, coughed, then set the glass aside.

Joseph simply gaped at her.

Before he could begin to recover, she asked, "Are you having an affair with Millicent Switzer?"

He sighed. He didn't like explaining himself twice. He'd done nothing wrong. "No, Elise. I told you earlier Millie is naturally upset about Gilbert's death. She's worried about the boys. She turned to me as a friend. Nothing more."

"Maybe on your part. She looks at you much differently, however."

He'd never thought that himself until today. But he'd seen a look in Millie's eyes earlier that wasn't about friendship. "Don't be ridiculous," he said to his wife, knowing Millie would get past her...whatever to him. He didn't want this brought into his house.

"She wants you."

His face heated. Where had Elise gotten this frank talk? "She's a friend. Nothing more."

"You dated once."

"Are you implying I never got over her, or I want to see her again?"

"Either. I won't have this family go through the kind of humiliation Gilbert brought down on his."

"Which is all the more reason why I would never do anything like that!" He rose, deliberately using his height to intimidate her. "I don't have any feelings for Millie beyond as a friend and client. I married you. We made a life and a family together. I have no regrets about the choices I made."

"Then prove it."

"Prove—" He swallowed his anger, as new, unfamiliar emotions pushed against him. *Doubt. Worry.* Could Elise actually be jealous? And what would she do if these unfounded thoughts festered? "What do you expect me to do?"

"Stay away from her. She can confide in her priest. She can—" she bared her teeth "—*hug* another friend."

"We've been friends for more than thirty years. *You've* been friends for almost that long."

"And we will be again…once she finds another man to *hug.*"

"I'm processing her husband's will. I can't not take her calls." Not to mention she was one of only two people besides himself who knew the details about the second will. Unless you counted the possibility of a stripper from Daytona Beach. Which he didn't.

Elise leaned across the desk, her eyes bright with fury. "Calls, fine. Visits, no."

"I won't have my wife dictating my professional obligations."

"Then you can make other plans during our usual Wednesday-night appointment."

She was withholding sex? What the devil had gotten into the woman? "Are you threatening me?"

"No, Joseph. I'm *telling* you. Get rid of that woman." She turned and strode from the office, closing the door behind her with a decisive snap.

Incredulous, he sank into his chair. He tossed back the drink he'd poured, then winced at the burn down his throat. Scotch was to be sipped, savored. Like life.

His life had been perfect a few weeks ago. Exactly as it should be. Damn Gilbert Switzer for dying. This was all that bastard's fault. Why couldn't he have hired an upscale escort service, like every other normal man? Though Joseph had never availed himself of their services, he had several on file in case a visiting colleague or client had the need.

How many empires had fallen because of somebody's stupid dick?

As much as he wanted to call Elise's bluff, he knew he wouldn't. She fought dirty. He ought to know; he'd taught her.

Though he wasn't overly demonstrative, he loved his wife, the comfort and companionship she gave him. She was reserved herself. Their goals and personalities suited each other. Their life together was important to him, and he wasn't going to let anyone or anything threaten that.

Come to think of it, Millie's over-the-top emotions were another reason he'd broken off their relationship.

He looked at the grandfather clock against the wall. After ten. Too late to call. He'd leave it till morning.

Somebody had to help him out of this mess. And he had the ideal person in mind.

AFTER SOME PREP for that evening's catering job, Vanessa dressed carefully for her lunch with Lucas. She slid into a black silk camisole and fitted black pants, paired with a white blazer. For luck, she wore her lacy red bra and matching panties underneath. For confidence, she wore sky-high black stiletto sandals.

At eleven-thirty on Saturday morning.

"Is this how hookers prepare for the day?" she asked her reflection—which didn't look half-bad—then rolled her eyes at herself.

She was still vaguely annoyed—and aroused—by Lucas's abrupt departure the night before, but after some solid hours of sleep, she had to admit she had a clearer mind and a new perspective on their relationship.

Namely, to find out just what their relationship was.

Were they dating? Were they casually screwing each other? Were they confidants? Friends? A combination of everything?

Since meeting him, she'd run the gamut of emotions. Were these complex feelings cosmic payback for the relatively uncomplicated relationships she'd enjoyed over the past couple of years?

Last night had brought *some* comfort, at least. Lucas definitely wasn't using her to get back at her father, or to get to know her father. She had to unpack that baggage.

Especially since Lucas seemed to have plenty of stuffed suitcases of his own.

No matter how she looked at it, she still felt as though they were on opposite sides of a very high fence. Being a practical girl, she was pretty sure a couple dozen sweaty encounters between the sheets would fix that—at least temporarily. Hence, the outfit.

After that, however, she had no idea where to go. Did she need to know? If she was going to risk the possibility of peace and renewal with her relatives, it seemed as though she should.

Still, a girl's gotta do...

"That's *woman*," she said as she dabbed spicy Asian perfume between her breasts.

As she headed toward the door, her phone rang. One glance at caller ID and she winced. Her father.

She considered ignoring it but knew he'd just call her cell, which she always kept with her. A woman who planned, cooked and served at important social events for other people didn't have the luxury of being incommunicado.

She snatched the cordless receiver off the charger. "Hi, Dad."

"I hope you don't answer your business line like that."

"Of course not. I say *Have Dessert First.*"

Silence. Then he said, "I'm not sure that's appropriate either."

"Did you need something? I'm on my way out."

"Where?"

As if she were still sixteen. "An appointment. Is everything okay?"

He cleared his throat.

Hesitancy from her father? Clearly, everything was *not* okay.

"I'd like to ask a favor," he said.

Knees weak, Vanessa sank to the edge of her bed. Ridiculously, she wondered if her mother knew. Or had Mother put him up to this request? What was going on with them? Her mother asking Vanessa to bail her out using the cooking skills she didn't even like to acknowledge her daughter possessed, and her father asking for a favor? Her father didn't even like to ask someone to pass the peas at the dinner table. Self-reliance—and even sometimes self-centeredness—was his motto.

As a result, he wasn't overly demonstrative. And while she and her father had always gotten along better than she had with her mother, they weren't really close. Maybe because she'd always wished he'd been a buffer of comfort and acceptance between her and the imposing, demanding Elise Douglas, but he'd never come through.

"Okay," she said finally, glad her voice didn't shake.

"As you may have heard, Millicent Switzer lost her husband recently. And she's been a bit lonely. You know a variety of people, so I thought you might…know someone who could maybe…"

"You want me to be a pimp for your old girlfriend?" she asked, incredulous.

Surprisingly, *pimp* was not the word he jumped on. Vanessa didn't know whether she was more worried by that or not.

"She's not my old girlfriend," her father said, his voice rising with censure.

"Come on, Grandma told me all about you two."

Silence again. "We dated for a brief period many years ago. The important thing here is that she needs companionship. She's been through a trying time the last few weeks, and I'd like to do what I can for her."

As much as she'd like to give her father a hard time, she felt sorry for him. Maybe he didn't know the meaning of the word *pimp*. Maybe he finally realized the arm's length where he held everybody was a little too far away.

Also, she did know who Millie Switzer was. Millie's husband was a dog, who'd publicly humiliated her and her sons with his not-so-private affair with a stripper.

"And she needs a date," she said.

"Just a distraction," her father said quickly, as if sensing he'd won.

Thinking of the bachelorette party, which was for a client/friend, she decided *that* would certainly be a distraction. Maybe not a Daddy-approved distraction, but, hey, a man who didn't know the actual duties of a pimp had to take what he could get. "I'm sure I can come up with something. Do you have her numbers?"

Her father gave her all the contact info, and she signed off without asking how everything was with him. Until she could work out what she was going to do with—and *to*—Lucas, she wanted to keep a low profile with her parents. Running from a fight wasn't her usual mode of operation, but when a woman was vulnerable *and* horny, she tended to not to have the best judgment.

By the time she reached Lucas's high-rise office building, nerves had taken over. She searched for bold and came up empty. She gathered her confidence and found only wobbly ankles in overly high shoes.

Still, she moved through the lobby and gave her name to the receptionist, who waved her toward the elevator.

When Vanessa walked into his office, she noted a sleek, glass-topped desk on one side and a formal furniture grouping and full bar on the other. He was standing at a huge window that looked out over the city, just as she'd imagined him doing in his apartment. As always, something solitary surrounded him, held him apart.

He glanced over his shoulder at her, then smiled briefly. "Have a seat."

Really apprehensive now, she slid into one of the black leather chairs in front of his desk. The office was modern and glossy. Cold, almost. The gray, black and white decor communicated impersonal strength. Was this really him, or the image he wanted to portray?

He finally turned and approached his desk. "You look beautiful," he said as he stopped next to his chair.

But he hadn't touched her. Didn't he want to?

"Thank you."

"You slept well?"

"Yes." He, on the other hand, looked as though he hadn't. The fatigue in his eyes only added to his masculine appeal, but she wondered if all his time with her had cut into some project he was working on, if he'd worked long into the night to catch up. "Lucas, are you sure you're—"

"I was raised in a trailer park in Lafayette, Louisiana."

She swallowed as their eyes met. She'd asked for this. As much as the practical side of her knew she had to hear it all, the head-over-heels side of her wanted to stop him. She stood. "Lucas, don't."

"We can't go forward without you knowing the whole story."

"I guess not." She returned to her seat, but the knot in her stomach grew.

"My only request is that you not repeat what I'm telling you to anyone but Mia. My…reputation, such as it is, is something I've cultivated carefully. It's important that it remain intact."

Did he mean some of the rumors were true? Or were they false, and he'd deliberately not corrected them? "Agreed."

"So." He smiled without humor. "We go back to the trailer park in Lafayette…

"My parents weren't exactly pillars of the community. My father was a thief, and not a good one, given our living conditions. My mother was hooked on pills and alcohol."

Vanessa sat very still, trying not to let her pity show. And she'd complained—frequently—about the opulent surroundings where she'd been raised.

"Neither of them had much time for an energetic, then troublemaking kid. By the time I was sixteen, I'd gotten into some trouble, did a couple stints in juvie and figured out the old man had one thing right—take all you can, and do it before somebody else does. I started my big-time career as a criminal by stealing a car."

She couldn't suppress a wince this time.

"Ah, but that turned out to be the best move I'd ever made, since I got arrested."

He began to pace. "The judge and jury realized juvie wasn't doing me any good, so I was indicted and ordered to stand trial as an adult. The court appointed me a lawyer. An older guy who'd seen way too many punks like me. He was just ready to retire." Lucas stopped to look out the window. "But he saved me. I'm not sure why and to this day he isn't either. He told me if I stayed out of trouble and graduated, he'd find a way to get me into college.

"Ridiculous as it sounds, I felt as if heaven had opened and let me finally peak at what lay beyond its golden gates. I took the deal. Soon after, my father was arrested on burglary charges and later sentenced to fifteen years. He blamed me until the day he died, said I'd ratted him out."

"Did you?"

"No, but I'm sure it was my lawyer's doing, so I was essentially the cause. I didn't cry any tears over him, *chère,* and he died in prison a few years later."

Vanessa knew better than to say she was sorry. "What happened to your mother?"

"My lawyer tried to get her into rehab, but she wouldn't stay. Years later, I bribed her with a house if she'd get clean, which she did for about three months. It's a routine for us now. Every so often she calls me for money and I dangle the rehab as bait." He shook his head. "But back then she lost custody, and I was handed over to the gentle nuns of St. Francis, where I lived and finished high school.

"Once I applied myself, a strange thing happened…I succeeded. I got a scholarship to Tulane and moved to New Orleans."

"And you succeeded there, too."

He walked around the desk to lean against it, close enough that his leg brushed her knee. "Yes," he said, staring down at her with an odd mixture of need and self-deprecation. "I worked in a bar in the French Quarter. I found not just bravado, but confidence. I graduated, went to law school, passed the bar. Along the way, I learned another important thing about myself. I learned I could read people, then play people. I could get them to do what I wanted, to see my side of a case. I'd found my niche—which I used to advantage. Female jurists flirted with me. Male jurists considered me strong and sincere. I felt none of it. I had a Porsche, a seven-figure income and no conscience.

"I was there to win. I wanted the judgment. The glory. The respect. The *check,*" he added as if to bring home the point.

She met his gaze, not judging him as he undoubtedly expected her to do. She might have grown up wealthy, but she had some idea of what it meant to be poor and hopeless. "So you became a success and earned a lot of money, but last night you said you were atoning. For what?"

"One of my first big judgments involved a woman who had cancer. Her insurance company fraudulently denied her health coverage, claiming a preexisting condition. I sued, on her behalf, for fifteen million dollars. It was an easy win. The insurance company bigwigs were idiots. Memos all over the place about systematically denying her coverage, so they didn't have to fork over the bucks for her treatments.

"My fee for her pain and suffering was nearly five million dollars." His voice deepened, quieted. "After the decision came down, I bought Cristal and got drunk. She resumed chemotherapy."

"You couldn't have cured her cancer, Lucas."

He went on as if he hadn't heard her. "Six months later, she died, leaving a devastated husband and young daughter. I didn't even go to the funeral. I sent flowers. I'd already moved on to the next case." He shook himself before continuing. "Then several months ago, her daughter wrote me. She...thanked me. Said her father had gone through severe depression after her mother's death, but the money had helped pay for his treatment, and he was even dating again. Though she'd always miss her mother, the settlement money had allowed her to attend college. She wants to be an attorney, and she wanted to let me know that I'd been her inspiration."

"That's wonderful," she said, though she could see where this was going. "You helped that family."

His gaze was hard and cold. "I *used* her, Vanessa. When the case was referred to me, I saw that the insurance company was a local outfit. I figured on their lack of so-phistication and disorganization. But they had one very important thing going for them—for *me*—they were under-written by a deep-pocketed, bigger company. One I could sue for megabucks. Without that one catalyst, I would have passed off that family without another thought."

Vanessa wanted to flinch. He was deliberately giving her the brutal truth. So she would understand him? So she would blame him?

She kept her face impassive.

"I never thought of that young girl. Not *once*. I had to look her name up in my records. Brittany Ann Curry. She was thirteen when her mother died. And do you know how many clients I've had just like that?" He bowed his head. "Too many to count.

"I had become my father, taking all I could," he said as he rolled his shoulders and met her gaze, his effort to escape the past and control his emotions obvious. "Somewhere along the line, the winning and the money and maybe my genes had taken over. I'd forgotten why I even became a lawyer in the first place—to help people who couldn't help themselves. So, I announced I was closing my practice and made plans to move here."

"Why here?"

"Brittany started law school at Emory this past spring. Since the day I got her letter I've been talking with her, offering study help and the perspective of a practicing attorney. I've learned she's smart and insightful, and so damn young and enthusiastic about defending truth and justice." He smiled sardonically. "I was never that optimistic or innocent, but I'm watching her and learning. She considers me her mentor. One day I hope to actually be worthy of the honor."

If he expected Vanessa to be appalled or to reject him, he was going to be disappointed. He'd gotten out of a dead-end life, and no matter what he thought, he had helped people.

Whatever happened between them from this day on, she'd always admire him. Who else had the strength and courage to examine his life with such brutal honesty? To make wholesale and painful changes to find a more meaningful purpose?

Though she'd never thought of herself as courageous, she'd made changes to follow her own dreams, to make a life that was her own, one she could be proud of. She'd never expected to meet someone she had something so deep and basic in common with.

Someday, she'd make sure to thank him for reminding her she'd done the right thing.

She realized now where the coldness inside him had sprung from. That didn't make it any less scary, but then so much about him was frightening for a woman intent on simply keeping her business afloat, repairing her relationship with her family and having a little fun along the way.

The way he made her feel scared her. How she felt when she wasn't with him. How much she already cared about him.

Praying her knees would hold her, she stood. "That's it?" She laid her hand lightly on his chest. "I thought you were in the Witness Protection program or something. What's for lunch?"

Still seeming distant, he just looked at her. "Aren't you worried I'm playing you?"

She wedged herself between his legs. "No."

"I'm not easy to get along with."

She slid her fingers through the hair at the nape of his neck. She reveled in the softness. "Neither am I."

"You don't care about the kind of man I am?"

"Of course I do." She traced her index finger along his lower lip. "You're smart. And interesting." She brought her face closer, so their lips were mere inches apart. "Flawed and strong. Gorgeous." She brushed her mouth over his. "Noble."

He tried to interrupt, so she kissed him again. "Brave. Fun. Charming."

"I don't need you to coddle me."

She smiled. "Yes, you do."

When she placed her mouth over his this time, she slid her tongue past his lips. She seduced him out of the past and into the present.

Part of her recognized she was falling back on their already familiar hunger and heat to block the feelings worming their way into her heart. If she only loved him with her body, she could prevent herself from caring too much. She treated her relationships casually out of a need for protection. She didn't have a great long-term record. Her rapport with family being exhibit number one.

Her reflections flew from her mind, though, as Lucas pulled her against him. He certainly knew how to read people, since he always found the spot on her that needed his touch the most. He knew whether to stroke softly or firmly, slowly or quickly.

Now, he savored her lips as if she were the finest champagne, as if knowing she wanted to offer him comfort and solace, a physical balm to heal the past. His arms encircled her. Her heart began the familiar pounding. Her stomach fluttered with desire.

She wanted his strength and intensity as much as she wanted to tap into his tenderness. His mouth was heaven. His body hard and strong, yearning to be explored. She craved the moment she could get him out of his respectable suit. Her fingers tingled with need. She wanted him inside her, under her, over her.

"You look incredible," he whispered hotly against her ear.

"So glad you noticed." She paused. "Finally."

He laughed, his breath brushing her skin, sending electric darts of pleasure shooting through her, ending between her legs. "Let me lock the door."

Vanessa raised her head as he moved away. She'd completely forgotten they were standing in his office in the middle of the day. The man cast some kind of spell—one she wasn't anxious to wake up from.

She should have been shocked by her behavior, or at least mildly embarrassed by her intense need. Instead, she wondered just how sturdy that desk of his was.

By the time he'd turned around, she'd shed her jacket and thought about taking off more, but decided she'd rather let him do the honors.

He pressed a button on the wall before he headed back toward her, and a set of curtains moved along the wall to black out the windows.

She glanced at the disappearing view. "Handy."

He yanked her back into his arms. "Isn't it?"

His hands and lips seemed to be everywhere at once, and she fought to adjust to the sudden change. With him, she felt off balance and steady at the same time. She wanted him, but not too close.

His revelations about his past intruded yet again. The physical and emotional hard times. The fear, pain and loneliness. The rise to the top, then the realization that he'd lost something important along the way. The need in his eyes for change, enlightenment and ultimate acceptance of himself.

She was both awed and frightened by his trust. She felt closer to him, making her doubt her vow and need to keep things light and fun between them. Could she close off her emotions just because she didn't want to get hurt? Could she find a way to blame her impulsive nature this time? When it was over, could she laugh and say, "Oh, well, it started with a one-night stand anyway"?

He trailed kisses down her neck, along her jaw, and she closed her eyes against thoughts and emotions too deep to explore. His hands molded her to his body. Clothes hit the floor. Before long, he was wearing only his pants, and she was down to her red bra, panties and stilettos.

The possessive, lustful way he looked at her made her shiver in anticipation. "You're every dream I've ever had come to life."

He wrapped one arm around her waist, then boosted her onto his desk. Watching her reaction, he drew his finger down her body, sliding it briefly beneath her bra, then moving down her stomach to the edge of her lacy panties.

He slid his hand inside, through the hair between her thighs, then diving into the heat and wetness. She let her head fall back as he pleasured her. She'd enjoyed other men, but had her needs ever been so powerful, so overwhelming? She wanted to indulge herself with him over and over, didn't want the sensations to end. She craved his touch, and delighted in the whispered words of encouragement and desire he rasped in her ear.

"You're are so hot…so beautiful," he said, his fingers moving faster, making her moan.

Her stomach tightened. Her breathing hitched. Every muscle in her body strained for the peak she was climbing. Then her hips bucked, and the ecstasy rocketed. She gasped and gripped the desk, while Lucas murmured in her ear.

Then before she'd even caught her breath, he'd ripped her panties off and was plunging inside her. "How? When—"

"I—" He struggled for breath and squeezed his eyes

shut. Pleasure rippled across his face. "I put a condom in my pocket earlier."

With him buried deep inside her, she braced her hands on his shoulders. "You did?"

"I'm learning it pays to be prepared with you."

A naughty grin spread across her face. She wrapped her legs around his hips and pulled him in even deeper. "Doesn't it, though?"

But he didn't smile, he moved.

He withdrew, then pushed in, setting a no-nonsense rhythm that was at odds with the long, sweet seduction they'd begun with. Need was chasing him, and maybe the demons of the past. She held on for the ride, knowing every moment she spent with him, every experience they shared, only added to their intimacy.

As he pounded against her, her lace-clad breasts slid against his chest, teasing her nipples to hardened peaks. Stimulation rocked the nerves at the center of her body and flowed outward, rippling pleasure down her spine and legs, helping her block out her worries. Nothing had changed. They were enjoying each other. For as long as it lasted.

Then why did she feel as if his heart were one with hers, beating in time, racing and chasing a satisfaction and completeness only he could give? Why was she suddenly sure she'd never truly had a connection until the moment Lucas had approached her two nights ago?

This thing between them was powerful enough to en-rapture her, to have her overriding all the caution she should feel about involvement with a lawyer, a competitor of her father's, a man who so quickly had embedded himself into her life. She'd risk a great deal to have Lucas.

Was it possible she was risking her heart?

She gripped a handful of his hair as his pace increased, and the euphoria surrounding her body shot to new heights. She opened her legs wider, adjusted the angle of her hips until she was sure he was pounding his way to her soul.

The first ripples of her orgasm tore through her, and she gasped. Her inner walls pulsed, squeezing him, bringing his own peak. He held her close, then his body bucked, bucked, bucked....

She dug her fingers into his shoulders as the waves of satisfaction rose and fell across her. Moaning, trying to calm her breathing, she collapsed against him. She wanted to say something sweet and tender, so, afraid of that inclination, she didn't.

She gripped his bare neck. "I needed that."

His chest rumbled. "Clearly."

7

LUCAS FOUGHT FOR BREATH as he clutched Vanessa against him. She was a remarkable woman, but he hadn't known how amazing until today.

He was spent, ridiculously happy and satisfied. He'd had a lifetime of hungering for achievement, for the next hurdle. What would become of him if he floated into contentment?

He'd gotten to the top and stayed there out of hunger. When he was full, where could he find the next challenge?

With Vanessa?

God knew a relationship with her wouldn't be easy, regardless of how far lust took them. They were very different people, with undoubtedly different outlooks on life. But he felt as if he were holding a fragile egg, a precious gift that—if nurtured—could grow into something miraculous, something way beyond what he'd ever hoped he'd have. Or deserve.

She didn't turn away.

After all he'd told her, she hadn't judged him or shunned him. Or even really asked why.

She'd just accepted.

An Important Message from the Editors

Dear Reader,

Because you've chosen to read one of our fine novels, we'd like to say "thank you"! And, as a special way to thank you, we're offering you a choice of two more of the books you love so well, and a surprise gift to send you – absolutely FREE!

Please enjoy them with our compliments...

Pam Powers

Peel off Seal and Place Inside...

FREE GIFT SEAL

THE EDITOR'S "THANK YOU" FREE GIFTS INCLUDE:

▶ 2 Romance OR 2 Suspense books

▶ An exciting surprise gift

YES! I have placed my Editor's "thank you" Free Gifts seal in the space provided at right. Please send me the 2 FREE books which I have selected, and my FREE Mystery Gift. I understand that I am under no obligation to purchase anything further, as explained on the back of this card.

PLACE FREE GIFTS SEAL HERE

▶ DETACH AND MAIL CARD TODAY! ▶

Check one:

| ROMANCE |
| 193 MDL EE39 393 MDL EE4M |

| SUSPENSE |
| 192 MDL EE4L 392 MDL EE4X |

FIRST NAME   LAST NAME

ADDRESS

APT.#   CITY

STATE/PROV.   ZIP/POSTAL CODE

(ED1-HQN-06) © 1998 MIRA BOOKS

The Reader Service — Here's How It Works:

He wasn't sure he deserved that kind of faith, but he craved it. Though he knew there was still much to explore and learn between them, he was glad he'd shared his past, his quest to make himself into a better man. He found himself wanting to reveal more, to share his fears and his hope for a future he could be proud of. To deepen their connection.

"I'm not part of your world, you know, *chère*. I just live there."

She leaned back and stared at him. "What are you talking about? My world?"

"My fine way of speaking, my manners and my sense of style are all just decorations. As you saw so vividly last night, I'll never be truly accepted by the wealthy and privileged."

"I couldn't care less. In case you haven't noticed, Mr. Broussard, I'm the black sheep in my family."

He kissed her temple. "Then we'll be outcasts together."

Pulling away, he zipped himself back into his pants, vaguely wondering if he should be ashamed that he'd just slammed the daughter of one of the most powerful attorneys in the South.

On his desk. In the middle of the day.

Some of those trailer-trash tendencies would probably never completely fade.

There was no repairing the panties, but he helped her gather the rest of her things and sent her into his private bathroom to freshen up, while he dressed. He also ordered lunch to be delivered from a Thai restaurant on the next block.

By the time she emerged from the bathroom, he'd opened a bottle of wine and reopened the curtains.

She walked out barefoot, her impossibly sexy shoes dangling from her fingertips, just as she had the morning she'd left his apartment. Was that only yesterday?

"I nearly swallowed my tongue when you walked in here earlier," he said as she settled on the other end of the sofa.

She accepted a glass of wine and eyed him over the rim. "You acted awfully cool."

"I was reciting statutes in my head to keep myself from jumping you."

She smiled. "Yeah?"

He patted the cushion next to him. "You're pretty far away down there."

"Wild things happen when we touch."

"I promise to restrain myself."

She grumbled, "It's not you I'm worried about." But she slid down the sofa, facing him, and draped herself across his lap. "Better?"

He stroked her hair off her face. "Much."

"Once, I brought a motorcycle-riding hooligan to one of my parents' Sunday dinners."

He raised his eyebrows. "Hooligan, huh?"

"Well, my mother called him that, not me."

"Is this a contest? To see who has the badder past?"

"No, you win hands down there. Just so you know my own past wasn't as idyllic as it might seem."

He was curious about how she'd become the black sheep, and how—given her father's reputation—he'd managed to raise such an interesting woman. "Go on."

"And what are we doing about lunch? We are *having* lunch, aren't we?"

He loved that she always thought with her stomach. "I ordered pad thai. It should be here any moment."

"Yum." She sipped her wine. "Now where was I?"

"Motorcycle-riding hooligan."

"Right." Lustily, she sighed. *"Justin."*

Jealousy stabbed him. He hoped wherever *Justin* was today it was near Outer Mongolia.

"Justin wasn't really a hooligan—whatever that is. He was just different. His dad was a big-time music producer, so he wasn't around much, and Justin had definitely seen *Rebel Without a Cause* one too many times, but I liked him."

"Joseph and Elise thought differently, I take it."

"Joseph and Elise live on an entirely different planet."

They were interrupted by the arrival of the food, but Vanessa continued her story as they shared the spicy noodle dish loaded with shrimp at the coffee table.

"Anyway, Mother was always nagging me about inviting *a nice boy* to dinner. 'How about that Middleton boy?'" she said in a high, formal tone that no doubt mimicked her mother's. "'Or Arthur Richardson's boy?' Naturally, Quint Middleton's father was a circuit court judge and Richardson was dean of the business school at Georgia Tech."

She wrinkled her nose to communicate what she thought about that. "Boring and pompous. I liked Justin, so I invited him."

"You had to know that wasn't going to go over well."

"Yeah, I guess. I was young and reckless. And I figured

I'd just get grounded or something. I had no idea Justin would be the one punished."

"By your parents?"

"By everybody. They were *horrible* to him. They made demeaning comments about his hair, his leather jacket, his earring. They giggled behind his back, then to his face."

Lucas had experienced that kind of painful shunning himself. Both as a poor teenager and as a grown man—the dignified New Orleans set had only been slightly more accepting than the Atlanta country clubbers. Though the Crescent City crowd had eventually softened. Most of them respected a true scoundrel, after all.

"Needless to say, you won't be meeting my parents anytime soon. I won't put you through that."

"I'm not a sixteen-year-old boy, Vanessa. I can handle your parents."

"I guess. Just don't be offended when I don't invite you to dinner tomorrow."

"You still go?"

"Sometimes. But I don't bring dates."

"I'll endeavor to hide my disappointment."

"I am surprised you haven't asked me about them yet."

"What about them?"

"How Joseph Douglas's daughter wound up as a caterer in a barely respectable neighborhood with an empty bank account."

He'd figured there'd been a falling out, and he didn't expect she was catering as a charity project. But his curiosity about her was also connected to his thirst for information about her father and his "two wills" moral dilemma.

How could Lucas separate his needs, keep what he considered a legal secret and still learn all he wanted about Vanessa? He'd just have to find a way. He wanted to know what had happened along the way that had kept her from turning into those women he'd met Thursday night.

"Tell me," he said.

"I never really made much of a debutante. I'm not quiet, demure or traditional. I don't like lacy dresses, flat shoes or having my hair cut in a bob. I liked the sycamore tree in proximity to my bedroom so I could sneak out, the Mercedes my father gave me for high-school graduation and the unconventional friends I'd made.

"During my junior year in college, I was living at home and going to Emory. In my infinite wisdom, I decided to wear a white shirt to a ladies' luncheon my mother and I had been invited to. I also decided to wear a red bra underneath the shirt."

Lucas swallowed a mouthful of noodles. "You should have worn it to the *men's* luncheon. You'd have made a better impression there."

Her eyes twinkled. "If I'd only had you for inspiration. Well, you can imagine how my mother felt about my lingerie selection. When we got home, of course, we got into a huge argument. I was embarrassing my family, I wasn't living up to my obligations as a Douglas, I respected nobody's wishes but my own, et cetera.

"I listened, I apologized, and, when she left my room, I packed. I left that same night and moved in with a friend from school. Of course, I wasn't a complete martyr." She winked at him. "I did take the Mercedes. I got a job as a waitress when my parents, predictably, cut off all financial support. We rarely spoke over the next several months, and at the end of the school year, I went to my career counselor and told her I needed a new direction. She advised me to leave school."

"That must have been some counseling session."

"Temporarily, of course, though I never did go back to Emory. She told me to take a year off and work and think about what I wanted to do, what I really enjoyed doing. I figured out pretty quickly that I enjoyed working at the restaurant—the craziness, the ever-changing customers and menus. I eventually became a sous chef, then I got into the CIA—that's Culinary Institute of America. After I graduated, Mia and I decided to open Dessert First, and one day I realized I was actually happy."

"So you repaired your relationship with your family."

Shadows darted through her eyes. "Not exactly. My sister and I do okay, but my parents don't approve of my catering, or of me. Until Thursday night, I'd never gotten business from Mother. In fact, she's gone out of her way to steer people away."

Lucas fought to keep his voice even as anger rolled through him. "So why were you at the fund-raiser?"

"Mother's caterer canceled on her a few days before the event. She called me in desperation."

"You bailed her out even though she'd tried to sabotage you in the past?"

She looked startled. "She didn't sabotage me. She just didn't help."

"Hoping you'd fail."

"And come crawling back, I'm sure." She shook her head. "Like *that's* going to happen."

Lucas rose and poured more wine. As he sipped, though, he knew he was too furious to appreciate the delicate flavor, so he set the glass aside. "*I'll* hire you. And recommend you. Hell, I'll stand on the street corner and pass out your business cards if you need me to."

She glanced up at him. "That's really sweet, but I'm fine. Some months it's a struggle, but—"

"Don't you think it's odd that I've known you two days, and I'm willing to do whatever's necessary to help you succeed, and your own mother does nothing?"

Vanessa jumped to her feet. "Look, Lucas, I know it sounds awful, but it's not. I'm doing this on my own. I wouldn't have it any other way."

"On your own is entirely different from steering people away. I would have told her to screw off if she called me for help at the last minute."

Her eyes turned glacial. "She's my mother."

"Exactly. What kind of mother—" He stopped, turning away as he caught the stricken look on her face. Sometime in the last few seconds he'd gone from being angry at her mother to being angry at his own. "I'm sorry," he said quietly. "I have no place criticizing your family." *Especially since I have no idea how a good one is supposed to behave anyway.*

She wrapped her hand around his arm. "It's okay. It's sweet of you to want to defend me." She urged him to face her. "I have a weird relationship with my family, but I hope it won't always be that way. My mother's call felt like an olive branch, not a family obligation."

"Your family should appreciate you more. They should support you."

She grinned. "You tell them that when you meet them. You'll be a big hit."

He decided not to remind her she'd said he wasn't meeting them anytime soon. "I look forward to it."

She glanced at her watch. "I should get going. I have a bachelorette party to—" She stopped. "Damn. The favor. I need to make a quick call."

"Sure. I'll clean up."

While she pulled out her cell phone, he thought about all they'd told each other. They were a lot alike—breaking out of the molds that had been preset for them.

He was more intrigued by her than ever, especially knowing how she'd broken away from her uptight parents.

Of course, he still hadn't been totally honest with her. He knew—or rather strongly suspected—her upstanding father had done something not so upstanding.

But that was a professional thing, right? Attorney to attorney privilege. Or at least courtesy.

Was it really right of him to judge a colleague? On top of that, he certainly didn't feel he had the right to rat him out to his daughter. Besides, he didn't even have anything concrete to report, except a dead guy named Switzer and an odd conversation with a drunk guy named Anthony. He was tempted to put his investigator on the research, but that felt as though he were giving the whole business too much weight.

Still, keeping his suspicions to himself seemed as if he were, well…lying to Vanessa.

"Now I'm catering *and* socialite-sitting," Vanessa said as she closed her phone.

He frowned. "Socialite-sitting?"

"My father asked me to keep his socialite ex-girlfriend busy tonight, which I decided to do by taking her to the bachelorette party I'm catering. He actually asked for a special favor, which is strange since whenever my mother rants about how I don't sufficiently fulfill my obligation to my family, whom I'm also usually embarrassing, he just sighs."

Lucas clenched his jaw, then said, "I really don't think I like your family."

"And you haven't even met Angelica yet. She'll probably call sometime this afternoon to try to set me up with one of her husband's doctor buddies, since she hasn't tried that in almost a week."

He wrapped his arms around her waist and pulled her close. He'd like to hold her tight and keep people from hurting her—and afterward inform her sister she was off the market to setups with doctors. "You shouldn't let them treat you this way."

"I know, but I'm so good at it."

"Vanessa, they—"

She laid her finger over his lips. "I know," she said, softer, unable to hide the hurt. "I need to get going. I have tons of prep to do, and Mia's at the lake. I'm sure Millie will take a frickin' limo to the party, so I'll have to—"

"Millie?"

"Switzer. My dad's old girlfriend."

Mrs. Switzer, she's so nice. A chill raced through him as he recalled Anthony's drunken compliment. *The widow.*

"You know her?" Vanessa asked, obviously noticing his curiosity.

"No, though her name sounds familiar."

"Her husband just died, and you may have heard the rumors about him."

He wished he could stop the urge to ask. "Rumors?"

"He was cheating on her with some stripper. It was one of those everybody-knew-but-nobody-talked-about things. She probably doesn't know whether to cry or open a bottle of champagne now that he's dead."

Cry. She's out a big hunk of change. Or maybe not…

His curiosity had just become a quest. He had to call his investigator, who also just happened to be his suspicious, smart-as-hell cousin. It was time to get to the bottom of this. Dancing around the truth with Vanessa wasn't acceptable.

"Jeez, I've really got to go." Vanessa pulled out of his arms and headed across the room. "Can I call you later?"

He followed her to the door. "How about you let me come with you tonight and help?" And *not* just because he wanted to meet Millie Switzer. He didn't want Vanessa to go. He didn't want the night to pass without them being together. But the way his motivations might be perceived if she knew about his investigation was troubling.

She turned toward him. "You want to help me cater?"

"Yes."

"I don't think the groom would be very happy about that. This is supposed to be girls only."

"I'm not a guest. I'm an assistant. It'll help me understand what you do."

"It's hard work. I really don't think—"

"How hard can it be?" He slid his hands into his pants pockets. "*Please.* Tipsy women. Naughty lingerie gifts. A stripper fighting a beer belly. I think I can handle it."

She smirked. "Okay. I'll pick you up at six." She slipped on her shoes, then opened the door. "I won't have to come to court with you, will I?"

"No."

"Thank God. Bo-ring. And that doesn't look hard at all, by the way. Standing around, reading notes, smiling at the jury." She sniffed. "Easy. Make sure you wear black pants, a white shirt and a black tie," she added.

Then she blew him a kiss and strode out.

Laughing, Lucas corked the leftover wine and stored it in the bar fridge. She was an adventure. How could her parents see faults and ignore her amazing strength?

They knew each other's bodies; they were learning each other's minds. Would they find trust and understanding? Would their similarities temper their differences?

Did any of that even matter when he wasn't even sure he deserved her?

"Is it always this hard?" Lucas asked as he laid another load of dirty dishes on the kitchen counter.

Vanessa stroked her hand down his broad chest. He made a luscious waiter. "Are you sure it's not hard because you watched Tonya strip down to her thong?"

"Somebody got naked? I was too busy filling champagne glasses and cutting a penis cake—a too realistic version, I might add—to notice."

"Bull." Vanessa smiled seductively up at him, letting her hand rest on his belt. "Should I…check?"

"Well…" He snaked one arm around her waist and jerked her against him, so she could feel—without a doubt—how much he was enjoying the party. "I think my excitement has more to do with your outfit than Tonya's, though the pink bow on the back of her thong was a lovely touch." He leaned down, flicking his tongue across her earlobe. "You didn't tell me you had a thing for studs and black leather."

Vanessa glanced down at herself. Leather, strapless, silver-studded bustier? *Check.* Tight leather mini? *Got it.* Fishnet hose and black patent stilettos? *Oh, yeah.* False eyelashes and over-the-top exotic makeup? *Present as requested.*

The costume aspect of their bachelorette parties had naturally been Mia's idea, and it worked wonders on uptight crowds where the hostess's goal was wild and fun. Mia had a whole collection of outfits that were presented to the client when booking her party. (Female clients only, of course. They were caterers, not hookers.)

Vanessa got a kick out of the dress up part and had told Mia she wanted the dominatrix-chick—as opposed to the client's other request of innocent angel—especially for Lucas.

"What can I say...I'm a chameleon."

He backed her against the counter. "I want you. *Now.*"

Loving her role as the leader, she patted his chest. "All in good time, my loyal assistant."

He pressed his erection against her. "Now," he said, his eyes reckless.

She waggled her finger at him. "Don't make me get out my whip."

"I think I'll risk it." He kissed the top of her bare shoulder. "Mmm. Your skin tastes really good." He licked her. "Like sugar cookies."

She pointed at her cleavage. "It's the sparkle powder."

He dropped his head back and groaned. "Please tell me you've applied that all over."

"A few important places."

Mia swung into the kitchen, the low thump of the bass following in her wake. "Those chicks are really into this." She glanced at them. "And you two need to cool it. They want another tray of Hpnotiq cocktails. And that penis cake is demolished." She smiled at Lucas as he winced. "Sorry."

"Women are vicious."

"I'll get the cocktails," Vanessa said, stepping away from Lucas. He was way too much of a distraction to have at work.

Her partner grinned. "I think they'd rather have Lucas."

Throwing both women a cocky smile, Lucas crossed to the fridge and pulled out the Hpnotiq liquor bottle. "Duty calls, I guess."

Vanessa took the bottle from him while Mia added fresh ice to a tray of martini glasses. "You just remember who brought you here, assistant boy."

"But Tonya and her pink thong—"

Vanessa grabbed him by his tie. "Will be wrapped around your neck if you complete that thought."

"I'm crazy about commanding women," he said, spinning Vanessa around so she could fill the glasses with the seductive blue liquor. From behind her, he added the lemon wedge garnishes.

The heat emanating from his body made Vanessa want to push against him, made her wish for privacy and endless hours to indulge in fantasy and lust. For a moment, she closed her eyes and breathed in the enticing, spicy scent of him.

"If we get drinks out quick," Mia said, "we might not have a revolt."

Vanessa felt her face flush. She was getting too wrapped up in Lucas. After she filled the tray, she handed it to him. "You're walking home if you flirt with those women."

He winked. "Yes, ma'am."

"You're enjoying this way too much."

"Oh, no, *chère,*" he said as he walked toward the door. "This is really hard work."

With another wink and a smile, he sailed out of the kitchen.

"God, he's beautiful."

Vanessa eyed her partner. "Don't think I won't put the whip on you either."

"Just promise me I get your outfit for my date with Colin on Tuesday." Her eyes danced. "It clearly has an *intoxicating* effect on men."

"I guess the lake trip went well." With the flurry of catering prep, she hadn't had the opportunity to ask about the big boating date.

Mia wiggled her pink satin-clad hips. "Ooh, la, la." Dressed in the good-girl outfit—a tight silk dress, gathered on the sides and boosting her friend's bosom to new heights—Mia embodied cheeky fun. The big pink bow holding back her ponytail did nothing to spoil the *I'm good, but not really innocent* costume.

"How did you get Lucas to trade a date for work?"

"He volunteered."

Mia's jaw dropped. "Maybe it's true love. I mean, who would trade dinner and clubbing for *this?*" As she flung her hand out, a cheer rose from the other room.

No doubt the stripper their client had requested they hire had dispensed with another piece of clothing. Vanessa only hoped Millie was keeping her clothes on.

At the start of the party, Vanessa had shamelessly pressed a cocktail glass in her hand, introduced her to the hostess, then darted off to deal with the appetizers.

Millie had gotten into the spirit of the party. After a woman had suffered through a cheating husband, then a dead husband, Vanessa figured she deserved any fun she could get.

So far, Millie hadn't pulled a Tonya routine, but Vanessa still hoped the woman didn't give details about the night to her father.

Focusing on Mia, Vanessa considered *true love*. She was hot for Lucas, enjoyed being with him, but love was way in the future. She had a business to keep afloat, and, hopefully, a family to repair.

She was having fun with Lucas and counting on nothing else. No matter how many times she had to tell her fluttering heart of that simple fact.

Mia snapped her fingers in front of Vanessa's face. "He volunteered."

"He wanted to see what my work was like," she said as she loaded a tray of chocolate-covered strawberries.

"He wanted to see your ass in that leather skirt."

Vanessa hefted the tray over her shoulder and headed toward the door. "Oh, no. I kept that a surprise."

"Don't forget it's mine on Tuesday," Mia called after her.

8

VANESSA ENTERED the living room and found the stripper down to his silky black shorts and half the women too busy fawning over Lucas to notice. The next time her lover came to work with her, it was going to be at the Sister Mary Katherine retirement party.

The stripper, on the other hand, was not heading toward a potbelly. Vanessa wished she could fully appreciate him, but with Lucas nearby to appreciate, the stripper didn't even come close to comparing.

He continued with his teasing, hip-swiveling dance as Vanessa set the tray of strawberries on the coffee table. Her body throbbed for Lucas, but she made polite conversation with several guests.

Conflicted desire consumed her thoughts. She wanted him alone, but she enjoyed watching him interact. She needed to touch him, but she liked reveling in the anticipation.

She loved the crinkles that formed at the corners of his eyes when he smiled. She was crazy about the way he watched her when she talked. He was genuinely interested in what she thought. He wasn't just waiting for her to be quiet so he could make his own point.

He'd swung into the role of server so easily she remembered he'd done it before, working his way through school as a bartender.

His smile drove her wild. Beneath that serious lawyer there was a fun-loving guy, one who might not get out too often, but who clearly wanted to run free. His desire to be with her, his instinct to protect her made her sigh, her heart flutter.

Though her practical side was reserving judgment, most of the rest of her was cheering in unison.

This guy is special.

As another cheer rose, she focused again on the party. Millie's eyes were a bit glazed as she smiled vaguely at Lucas delivering a fresh drink, but hopefully she wasn't brooding over her cheating husband.

After he made his sweep through the guests, Lucas swung his empty tray over his head and walked toward Vanessa.

She watched the stripper execute a hip swivel.

"He's gay," Lucas said.

"He's not. Mia asked. Though who'd care. He's really hot."

Lucas cast a sideways glance at her. The challenge in that look made her shiver. "He is, huh?"

She tucked her arm through his. "Well, pretty hot."

"Thanks for letting me come tonight."

"*Thanks?* Catering is exhausting, before, during and after a party. Don't you want to go back to your cushy office?"

"God, yes." He laid his hand over hers. "But I like watching you—and not just because of the black leather getup. You and Mia are experts at making things happen, at including everyone, making a gathering an *event*. I can't wait to see what you do for my party."

She glanced at him. "What party?"

"The one I'm giving at my apartment that you're catering."

"Have we signed a contract on this?"

"I think it was more of a handshake deal." He paused, then grinned. "Or maybe a kiss."

"Just where was this kiss?"

"You mean where did it take place, or what body part was involved?"

He was too much. But then she'd always been an advocate for excess. "Both."

"In my office earlier today, I said I wanted to hire you. The details on what I kissed afterward are a little fuzzy, though. Maybe we should have a reenactment?"

Vanessa glanced around at the cheering, singing, dancing women. They seemed content. "I think that can be arranged." She headed down the hall to the spare bedroom where the women had stored their purses.

Obviously getting into the spirit, Lucas shut and locked the door. "You are a naughty lady."

She laid her hand in the center of his chest, pressing him back against the door. "I'm the dominatrix-lady tonight, and you'd better behave." She stepped close, flicking her tongue across his bottom lip, then sinking her teeth in lightly. "You're only getting a taste," she whispered. "I have other business to finish."

He moaned like a man in pain. "As your lowly assistant, I only deserve a taste."

Pleased, she laid her mouth over his, pushing her tongue lazily past his lips. He tasted like icing, and she smiled inwardly at the picture of him dipping his finger into the cake he'd served. The heat between them roared to life. She curled her fingers into his shirt as need invaded her body.

He molded her against him as he seduced her mouth. She tried to maintain her playfully dominant role, though she felt the urge to let him enfold her in his warmth. Her sense of independence would never let that last, but the impulse was still there.

Sometimes she felt in awe of his interest and pursuit. Why her? How had she gotten involved with this fascinating man? Was it possible their attraction could last?

He'd shown no desire to change her, to always put his needs ahead of hers, as others had in the past. Would he someday? One day, would he be embarrassed to tell his friends and colleagues that her profession involved wearing a leather bustier from time to time? Would his desire to be respected among the wealthy and successful force him to someday apologize for her catering?

Someday? her incredulous libido asked. *Are you crazy? Let's just get through tonight.*

To the cheering ovation of her baser needs, she slid her hand down his chest, then cupped his erection.

He lifted his head and stared down at her, his eyes glittering. "Don't start something you're not prepared to finish."

She stroked him up, then down, pushing the pads of her fingers against his fly. "Oh, I'll finish you." She stroked again. "Eventually."

Then she removed her hand and stepped back.

While he was momentarily stunned, she unlocked the door, then opened it.

His palm slammed against the door, forcing it closed again. "Are you crazy?" he asked, his voice strained.

She planted her hands on her hips. "No, I'm in charge."

A muscle along his jaw twitched. "Not anymore."

Quickly switching tactics—from badass dominatrix to put-upon caterer—she said in mock horror, "I can't have sex in a client's house."

"I don't see why not."

All furious, frustrated six foot two inches of him loomed over her.

Excitement and power washed over her. "Later, baby." She kissed him lightly. "It'll be worth the wait." She tugged on the door, and he moved his hand. She scooted out before he came to his senses.

Wow, there might be something to this dominant-chick deal. Not to mention revenge was sweet after he'd left her wanting last night.

She swallowed her smile as she heard him banging— what she presumed to be his head or his fist—against the wall.

THE TEASING, CONNIVING, winking, hip-shaking, leather-clad woman was driving him insane.

She'd accidentally, on purpose brushed against him about four hundred times. She'd smiled at him, winked at him. She'd even cornered him in the kitchen once and kissed him until he was dizzy.

He wanted her so much, he was shaking.

He'd been a good sport all night—serving drinks, cake and appetizers. He'd distracted overenthusiastic guests when they'd tried to rip off the stripper's clothes before he was ready to expose his leopard-print thong. He'd reminded himself he was a gentleman. Several times. He'd even enjoyed Vanessa's commanding tone—and definitely the outfit—as well as the flirting.

At first.

Now, however, he was on the verge of exploding. Being desperate, he could also admit that part of his anxiousness stemmed from losing control. He liked being in charge, professionally and personally. With that leather bustier and some aggressive hands, Vanessa had snatched control away.

He wasn't sure he liked the sensation.

"Maybe I should have brought the chocolate fountain," she said, appearing at his side.

That would have surely sent him over the edge. "I think it's time we moved these people along and packed up."

"But the client is having so much fun."

Dear God, that leather top boosted her bust to amazing heights. "Tell her I'll give her a thousand dollars to send everybody home."

She patted his cheek. "Poor Lucas. Is he frustrated?"

"You are a cruel and heartless woman, Vanessa Douglas."

"I know."

"Thank you so much, Vanessa," Millie Switzer said as she approached them. "This is a great party."

Tipsy, but not one of the women who'd attempted to jump the stripper, the widow Switzer smiled her appreciation.

Lucas had tried to avoid her during the night, but with a party of only twelve, that wasn't easy. He'd found himself forming the impression of a lovely but lonely woman, unsure how to act or handle the crisis in her life.

"I'm so glad you came," Vanessa said to Millie. "A girls' night out is just what you needed."

Millie's gaze slid to the stripper, who'd thrown a towel around his waist and was drinking a bottle of water, while surrounded by most of the other guests. "I wonder if this is how it happened for Gilbert."

The cheating husband. Suddenly Lucas didn't want to know about any of this. Why couldn't that idiot Anthony have kept his mouth shut? Why couldn't Lucas put the whole business out of his mind? Was he really considering ratting out a colleague? Even one who treated his daughter badly? Especially since he himself had done many immoral things in pursuit of "justice."

"If he met her just like this," Millie continued. "At a party. What was it about her—"

"Millie," Vanessa broke in, "the party's wrapping up. Why don't you get your purse, and we'll get you to your car."

Millie sighed as if she couldn't care less. "Yeah, okay." Listless, she ambled off.

"Men are pigs."

"*Some* men," he clarified, urging Vanessa toward the kitchen. "Let's start packing."

It took them nearly an hour, during which they cleaned both the kitchen and the living room, packed equipment and sent guests home in cabs or turned them over to Millie's steady limo driver. On the way home, Colin called

Mia, and they arranged to meet at the bakery. Recognizing opportunity, Lucas asked Mia to drop him and Vanessa off at his apartment, since she had Colin to help her unpack the van.

Surprisingly, Vanessa didn't argue against this plan.

Which was how he found himself unlocking his apartment door minutes later with his own personal dominatrix at his side.

He didn't bother to turn on any lights. He just tossed his keys on the foyer table, grabbed her hand and led her down the hall to his bedroom.

"I'm supposed to be in charge," she said.

"You can be on top."

His weakened knees lasted until he sat on the edge of the bed. She stood in front of him, hands on her hips, legs braced apart.

He allowed himself one, sweet, leisurely look down the length of her. From her glittery eyes and makeup to her overflowing bustline, to her tight mini that revealed miles of slender legs.

Perfection.

Part of him wanted to examine why he was so desperate for her. Though his body was incinerating itself from within, it wasn't just any woman he wanted. Not just any woman would calm the fever.

Only Vanessa.

She was an addiction, as necessary to him drawing the next breath as oxygen. Would he ever get enough?

As fire scorched his skin, and his heart threatened to leap from his chest, he lifted her skirt, grabbed the edge of her panties and yanked down. During the party he'd been perilously close to begging for relief, and now he was almost there….

He tugged her into his lap. When her crotch connected with his aching erection, he moaned, though that still wasn't enough. *In a minute, in just a moment, I'll be inside her….*

"That's two pairs of panties you owe me," she said, though her aroused eyes belied her casual words.

"Send me a bill." He had finesse. He really did. Where did it go when he touched her?

He fumbled with his fly, but somehow managed to roll on a condom.

Just another second…

His hands shook. Then, with a lift of her hips, she sank down, taking him inside her, sending ecstasy shooting down his spine. Her leather skirt rubbed against his stomach, and he wished he'd taken the time to get rid of his shirt, so he could feel the smooth material against his skin.

Vanessa rocked her hips and moaned deeply. But Lucas hadn't anticipated the control their position would give her, and she was moving way too slowly for him. He wanted to thrust deep, to satisfy the gnawing ache he'd endured all night.

"Faster," he muttered against her neck. "You've teased me all night."

She pushed him back on the bed. "Do you think we'll ever do this naked again?"

"Sure. In about ten minutes."

Obviously noting the desperation in his voice, she braced her hands on either side of him and increased her pace. No teasing rolls, no slow withdrawal and return. She banged against him, pistoning her hips as if she were running a race. Their mating was intense, and his stomach contracted with renewed lust.

Reaching beneath her skirt, he gripped her hips. She was determined, almost rough, and wildly exciting. He fought to hold back his orgasm until she came with him.

Then her thrusts suddenly sped up, she moaned, and he felt her contract around his erection. Stars burst inside his head, and he squeezed his eyes shut as his climax shot through him. His muscles contracted, his hips surged up. He shuddered one last time before his hands fell limply at his sides. Vanessa collapsed on top of him.

Minutes later, when his heartbeat had slowed closer to normal, when the chase of satisfaction was temporarily sated, regret rolled through him. He was trying to become the man he'd pretended to be for so long. He wanted to be respected for his character, not just his money and success.

And yet, when his needs had demanded, he'd done what he always had—he'd taken.

"Are you okay?" he asked. What if he'd hurt her? He recalled her climax just before his, but what if he'd been too rough?

"I'm hot."

"I can—"

She raised up and unhooked the bustier, tossed it aside, then, naked from the waist up, flopped back down on his chest as if undressing had been exhausting. "One thing's for sure, if we're going to keep doing this, I need to keep some spare undies in my purse."

His pulse stuttered. She obviously had no idea how much her easy, satisfied tone relieved him. "*Are* we going to keep doing this?" he asked quietly.

She rolled to her side and pushed her tangled hair away from her face. "If you want to."

He mirrored her position, trying to seem as calm and casual as she was, though he felt anything but composed. "I do. You?"

"I'm pretty lousy at relationships, Lucas," she said with a flip of her hand as her gaze darted away. "I get busy with my business and have to break dates. I keep weird hours and can rarely go out on the weekends. Plus, I'm trying to find a way to have some sort of normal relationship with my family, and that takes time and attention."

That old people-reading skill saved him once again, allowing him to see through her "busy" excuse. To see that her words and gestures were practiced.

It was possible she really didn't feel as intensely as he did, but he didn't think so. He'd acquired and cultivated arrogance, but he'd never been delusional, after all.

Still, he recognized that he'd met Vanessa at the worst possible time—when he was weak and vulnerable and unsure. He had time commitments of his own, professionally at his new job and some pro bono clients he'd taken on, personally in mentoring Brittany. He had miles to go to prove himself and make amends. Just how far, he wasn't sure.

Yet none of that mattered. He wanted Vanessa. To hold and enjoy, cherish and...love?

He would do whatever he had to to have her. Wasn't tonight's wild loss of control conclusive evidence of that?

Part of him was afraid of the road ahead. Part of him was exhilarated. And challenged.

He wanted her to want him as much as he did her. Letting her see the intensity of his feelings, though, wasn't the way to her heart. Plain and simple... Vanessa had been rejected by her family and was afraid of anybody else rejecting her again. He'd bet she deliberately broke dates and lost interest in relationships. Rejecting the guy before he could do the same to her.

Was it really that simple? To see her truth, maybe. To solve the problem it presented him? No damn way.

Keep it casual. No pressure, his instincts urged. Figuring out how to hold on to her would probably be a daily problem, but he would find a way around it. Through it, over it or under it.

He cupped her cheek, and he saw the longing reflected in her blue eyes. "I don't need all your attention. Just some of it."

Though obviously hesitant, she nodded. "I'll try."

"Then come with me." He slid off the bed, crossed briefly to the bedside table for condoms, which he slid into his pants pocket, then held out his hand to her.

She took it, and he led her into the bathroom. He slid the track lighting lever up just a notch, illuminating the huge shower with a soft spotlight. The spa quality of the shower was one of the reasons he'd settled on this apartment.

Moss-green tile covered the floor and walls: a glass enclosure surrounded the shower on three sides, and multiple nozzles jetted from the back wall. It reminded him of the breathtaking waterfalls he'd seen in Hawaii.

"That is some shower. I meant to tell you that the other night."

"You did say you wanted to get naked." He crossed the room and reached inside the shower to start the water. She should have looked ridiculous, standing in the bathroom, bare chested, wearing a leather skirt and sexy stilettos. But she didn't. She looked vulnerable and curious. A beautiful contrast of purity and naughtiness.

He began unbuttoning his shirt, and she bent to take off her shoes. She stumbled, and he darted to her side. "Let me." He helped her out of the shoes, then glanced up. "There, isn't that—"

The look on her face stopped him. The uncertain expression was gone, replaced by longing, a raw need that seemed just out of reach.

He rose, gripping her hand. "What?"

"Nothing." She blinked as if coming out of a spell. "You're pretty terrific."

Keep it casual. He waggled his eyebrows. "And you haven't even seen my soaping technique."

She laid her hands on his shoulders, underneath his shirt, then pushed it down his arms. "I can't wait." She closed the bit of distance between them so their bare chests brushed.

Steam floated around them, and the low light emphasized the intimacy. They undressed each other slowly, pausing for lingering kisses, featherlike touches. Lucas reveled in the incredible softness and delicacy of her skin. With her sass and strength, he wasn't always mindful of her fragility, of the elegant beauty he'd first seen in her.

But as he caressed her body and absorbed her touch in

return, the moment he'd seen her at the country club, red dress slithering over her body, came back to him. He'd been irresistibly drawn to her from the start. He wondered if he always would be.

Taking her hand, he led her to the shower, and his sassy lady returned in a snap.

She eyed the multiple nozzles shooting water at several angles. "That first night I was here, I didn't know how to work all the knobs. I mean, this thing has an electronic keypad, for God's sake."

The shower was so large, he could stand back and not get wet. After setting the condoms on the bench at the back, he nudged her toward the sprays. "Try it out."

"Aren't you coming with me?"

"In a minute." He wanted to watch her expression as the crisscross spray hit her for the first time.

She stepped forward without hesitation, straight into the middle. Instantly, she groaned, letting her head fall back. "Oh, my."

Watching the water sluice down her naked, silky body, pounding her curves with a liquid massage, his body roared back to life. "Indeed. You can change the rhythm of the pulses, too." Which he did, with a couple of taps on the keypad.

She moaned again, closing her eyes and turning around.

He smiled wickedly, though she'd likely forgotten he was even there. "And the angle." Another few keystrokes.

This time she gasped. She braced one hand against the tiled wall.

Obviously, he'd managed to hit the right spot.

Her gaze shot to his. Her face was flushed with heat and desire. "That's...amazing."

"I figured you'd enjoy it."

Her head bobbed as she leaned into the spray jetting between her legs. "I want one."

After rolling on a condom, he crossed to her, yanking her into his arms. "Mine." And he didn't just mean the shower. "You have to come to me for your fix."

She threaded her fingers through his wet hair. "I can live with that."

Leaning forward, she kissed him, and the playful mood turned hungry. The water stimulation had obviously cranked up her desire. Touching her, looking at her, hell, just breathing the same air she did, excited him.

As the water streamed over them, her tongue tangled with his. She held him tight against her body, seducing him both with her touch and her palpable need for him.

"You feel incredible," he said in her ear.

She arched into him. "Yes, I do."

"Wanna feel better?"

Laying his hands at her waist, he turned her to face the wall. From behind her, with water rushing over his back, he cupped her breasts, pushing them up and together as his thumbs rolled over her nipples, tightening them to eager peaks. He liked having unfettered access to her body, with no clothes or sheets to deal with. She was his to possess, to tease, to pleasure.

Vanessa pushed her bottom against the impressive hard-on cozying up to her. The shower alone was orgasmic. With Lucas included, the experience shot off the charts.

His warm hands slid down her stomach, his fingers dipping into the pulsing need between her legs. Closing her eyes, she licked her lips. After their hard lovemaking earlier, his wet hands slowly and surely caressing her sex felt like heaven.

Her nipples tingled. Her thighs trembled.

He licked and kissed her neck, even as his fingers spread her wide, and found the vulnerable tip of her desire. He pulled at her clitoris, then rolled it between his fingers. The coil of need tightened low in her belly, the ache spreading outward until her breathing grew shallow, until she was sure she would never reach that peak.

"Lucas, please."

He slowed his pace, and she gasped in frustration. "How much do you want me?" he asked.

"A lot." The shimmering edges of climax started to fade as his pace continued to slow. He moved his finger off the throbbing button that promised ecstasy. "A whole lot."

He sank his teeth lightly into her earlobe. "You're not wearing your dominatrix gear now. *I'm* in charge."

If it was possible, her desire multiplied. "O-okay."

He tugged her nipples, and a sharp ache of longing pierced her stomach. "Only I can make you feel like this."

"Only you," she parroted, getting into the spirit of the submissive role, even as she wanted him to end the pleasurable torture, and as she remembered it was his commanding presence that had first sparked her interest. He was made for the part. She could easily imagine how juries had fallen at his feet.

"I'll be inside you when you come," he said, then he

blissfully glided his hand back between her legs. He inserted one finger, then two inside her.

As she jolted from the renewed pleasure, she arched against him, lifting her hands up and back to wrap them around his neck. He placed warm, wet kisses along her neck and shoulders. She wanted more of him, all of him, and though she was panting with need, she recognized his breathing was also uneven, and his erection was rock hard, pressing against her lower back. He had to be as delirious as she was.

She turned his face to hers. "Now."

His eyes liquid and dark, he said nothing, but as he pressed his lips to hers, he slid inside her.

She closed her eyes, spreading her legs farther as he gripped her hips. He withdrew until just the tip of his erection remained inside her, then he surged forward. She absorbed the jolt of satisfaction with a groan.

Their joining turned him on like a light. He caught fire, though water streamed over them. She braced her hands against the slick tile wall as he drove himself inside her. From this angle, his erection seemed longer, thicker, moving deeper within her than ever before.

She tried to concentrate on simply the carnality of pleasure and satisfaction. Of desire leading to climax.

But her damn conscience wouldn't let her. Memories gushed over her just like the shower. His reckless flirting at the country-club fund-raiser. His need for restitution over what he saw as mistakes in his past. His anger at the way her family pushed her away, then drew her close when they needed to meet their own obligations or needs.

In just a few short days, she'd come to rely on his companionship, his caring, his spotlight of her needs. The loneliness she sensed in him was reflected deep inside herself. As social and open as she was with most people, she recognized she held much of herself apart. Just as Lucas did.

She relished his understanding and acceptance. Could she burden him with the need for acceptance she wanted from her family? Should she put that much pressure on him? Did she trust him with that vulnerability?

When he'd knelt at her feet a few moments ago, a strange sensation had skipped over her heart. Something powerful and foreign. Something scary. But wonderful.

Could she trust that emotion? Was she willing to try?

Pleasure swamped her before she could answer herself. She relished the slap of Lucas's flesh against hers, the ripples of sensation flowing through her body, absorbing into her blood and literally becoming part of her.

The climax he'd staved off was coming, like a train approaching a downhill slide. She panted in an effort to bring it quicker, to make the tight coil finally break free.

Then, miraculously, it did.

Her body clamped down, then released, and waves of pleasure rolled on and on and on, pulsing with such intensity her legs nearly collapsed from under her. She was vaguely aware of Lucas driving hard into her as he came just behind her.

As he held her to him like a precious jewel. As the heat of his body warmed emotions she'd banished. As he made her question every protective device she'd ever constructed.

9

JOSEPH DOUGLAS SCOOPED a stack of letters off his desk. Nearly two weeks after the hospital fund-raiser, and he was still behind on thank-you notes. He'd just laid them in his briefcase when his secretary buzzed him on the intercom.

"Mr. Douglas, Anthony would like to speak to you before you go."

Stifling his irritation, Joseph said calmly, "Send him in."

Moments later, his law clerk, sweat beaded on his forehead, shuffled in. "M-Mr. Douglas, I'm sorry to disturb you. I just…" He stared at his feet.

Joseph closed his briefcase with a snap. "You just what?"

As expected, Anthony jumped at his commanding tone. "Well, sir, I had this dream that I—"

"You're going to tell me about your dreams?"

Anthony's gaze darted from side to side. "I *think* it was a dream."

Joseph sighed. He really didn't have time for this nonsense. Elise was going to be cross with him if he was late to dinner again. And it was Wednesday.

"See, I was talking to this guy from Miami the other night—"

"Is this in the dream or real?"

Anthony licked his lips. "I'm not sure. I mean, I did dream all this, but I sort of think some of it happened, too."

An incoherent, hallucinating law clerk. Just what he needed. "Continue."

"Well, we were talking about Mrs. Switzer."

Joseph narrowed his eyes. "You and the guy from Miami."

His head bobbed quickly. "Yes, s-sir. We talked about how she's so nice and how she doesn't deserve— I mean how she always calls me by name and everything."

"And did you discuss anything that might pertain to this office? Anything private?"

Anthony stared at the floor. "No, sir."

Which, of course, meant he had. *Damn.* Anthony had graduated at the top of his class. He had an excellent memory for judgments and precedents that could be used to benefit their clients. He was a premier researcher. He wasn't an idiot. Normally anyway. "Was there a reason you chose to discuss confidential details about a client?"

"I guess I wasn't thinking right."

"No, you most certainly weren't." Joseph braced his hands on his desk in an effort to keep from strangling him. "Does this person from Miami have a name?"

"I don't know, sir."

"Description?"

"Tall. Maybe six feet. Dark hair. Dressed really nice. And he had a funny way of talking."

"Like an accent?"

Clearly confused, Anthony frowned. "I guess."

"Where did this conversation take place?"

"Outside the club, at the last fund-raiser."

"You drank quite a bit that night, as I recall."

Anthony hung his head. "Yes, sir. I did."

Joseph didn't allow himself an outward reaction. He didn't allow himself to worry about this breach in his plans. Whatever an obviously drunken, babbling Anthony had said most likely hadn't made sense, or else had been forgotten by the man from Miami.

He picked up his briefcase and headed to the door. "Don't think anymore about it. I'm sure it was forgotten."

Anthony rushed ahead to hold open the door. "I'm sure it was."

Joseph glanced back before he left the office. "Keep your mouth shut from now on."

"Of course, sir. You can count on me, sir."

The fear in his eyes reminded Joseph of Vanessa. Simply because she was the opposite. She met commands with defiance. And damned if he didn't admire that.

She'd never babbled, much less apologized for doing so. He didn't like her slaving away at that bakery. He'd wanted so much more for her, but with the latest mess he'd fallen into, he could somehow appreciate her need to mold, create, sell, then dust the flour from her hands.

"Good night, Patricia," he said to his secretary before he walked down the hall. As he passed employees, he nodded, though his mind was already on the task ahead.

It would mean asking his daughter for another favor. She would help him. She was generous without fault, and he wished he could say that trait had come from him.

Mostly, he was unsure how his wife would feel about his request.

They'd agreed their daughter's career choice wasn't ideal some time ago, but he hadn't considered Vanessa's stubbornness. Familiar feelings for him. He'd carried on a century-long tradition himself and understood the need to prove oneself worthy. Didn't she deserve the same consideration?

Besides, hadn't Elise just used Vanessa's services when her regular caterer had canceled? She wouldn't dare question his right to do the same.

Though it *was* Wednesday.

Once he'd settled into his car, he called Vanessa.

"Hi, Dad," she said, her voice sounding far away.

"Do you have me on the speaker phone again?"

"I'm fine. How are you? And, yes, you're on the speaker phone."

Where did that girl get her smart-ass mouth? From him, no doubt. That attorney arrogance. He just didn't like when it was used against him. "Pick up the phone, Vanessa."

"No can do, Pops. I'm kneading dough for sweet rolls."

Pops? He sighed. Arrogance was one thing, insubordination another.

"Do you speak to all your customers this way?"

"You're not a customer."

"I am now. I'm coming by there to talk about a party I need you to cater for me."

She was silent for several moments. "Sure. Just come to the workroom."

Driving over was a better way to handle this, especially

given the dire circumstances. His reputation, his livelihood, his *identity* could be compromised by what he'd done. He was doing what was right to protect his client. This was the mantra he'd cling to.

Once inside the bakery, he slid past the counter of glistening sweets, then pushed through the swinging door to the back room. He'd been here a few times. As much as he hadn't approved of her opening the bakery, he'd felt he needed to make sure the facility was at least safe and that she hadn't been ripped off on the rent. Then he'd needed to test the merchandise. Which had led to more visits. And a rapidly expanding waistline.

His daughter was talented. Smart and business-savvy, but also sensitive and creative. He longed to share his thoughts with both Elise and Vanessa, but he'd gotten caught up in a case, and...

What case had that been anyway?

He found his daughter with her hands in a large bowl of dough. "Something smells good," he said when she glanced up at him with a cautious look on her face.

"I have a batch cooling on the counter over there if you want one," she said, nodding.

"Your mother will have dinner waiting."

"Of course."

Silence. Not that they'd ever been easy communicators, but the tension between them seemed to worsen every year.

"You said something about a party?" she asked.

"Yes." Relieved to be able to move on to the reason for his visit, he said, "I'm planning for about twenty to thirty people at our house on Friday. It's a professional gather-

ing, men only, so don't make any pink drinks or other sil-
liness."

"Men only? Don't you know any female lawyers?"

"Of course I do. We have four at the firm. I want this
to be just the men, though. Whiskey and cigars. A few hors
d'oeuvres. Everything elegant and simple."

Vanessa's head lurched up. "Cigars in the *house?* Does
Mother know?"

"We're celebrating a junior associate's promotion," he
said as if he hadn't heard her protest. At least as soon as
he figured out which associate to promote. There was a
bigger agenda for this party after all. Anthony's not-so-
mysterious confidant. Mr. Miami.

Or was it a man who'd be more likely to say *mon ami?*

"I need a cost estimate right away," he added.

"I already have a party to cater Friday night. That's
only two days from now, you know."

"Cancel. I'm family. This is more important."

She sighed, pulled the dough from the bowl and plopped
it onto the flour-strewn table. "I can't cancel. I *won't* cancel."

"Don't you have an assistant? Can you not do more
than one party a night?"

"I have a *partner,* and I'll check with her, then I'll get
back to you."

"I'll wait."

After pounding her fist into the dough, she wiped her
hands on a towel, then walked out of the room.

Joseph concentrated on the successful outcome of the
party and not the fact that his oldest daughter was trying
to fit *him* into *her* schedule. He longed for the days when
he could just ground her.

But he couldn't ignore the feeling blooming in his chest. The connection with his child, his eldest child. So many of his hopes and expectations had been laid at her door. How had his pressure shaped her? Had he pushed her to leave? To rebel?

At the moment, he didn't really care what had driven her away. He wanted to gather his daughter closer, to find a way to keep her from running in the other direction. How ironic that a potential professional disaster would cause him to leap toward a personal need.

When Vanessa returned a few minutes later, she stopped just inside the room and crossed her arms over her chest. "I can do it. I'll e-mail you a suggested menu with prices in the morning."

She didn't look or sound enthusiastic. His fault. He should have been more supportive. He'd deferred to his wife's wishes, comfortable with the idea that she knew their girls the best.

"I appreciate you moving so quickly on this," he said.

"You're welcome."

"I also have a favor to ask."

"This last-minute party *is* a favor."

"You might remember I'm your father, young lady."

"You might remember I'm a grown woman."

He said nothing.

Then, quietly she said, "I'm sorry. It's been a difficult day. What do you need?"

He started to apologize for his own abrupt tone, but held back. Admitting a mistake wasn't something he did often. "What do you know about a new attorney in town named Lucas Broussard?"

His daughter coughed. Several times.

"Are you all right, Vanessa?"

"I'm—" She coughed again. "I'm fine. Who were you asking about?"

"Lucas Broussard. He's just moved here from New Orleans."

"I— Hmm. I think I may have met him at the fundraiser at the club."

"Yes, he was there. I need you to ask your friends about him."

Her eyes widened. "My friends?"

"He's close to your age, and I need to know what he's like."

"Why?"

"I'm inviting him to the party, just to welcome him to town. He's part of our legal community now."

"I see." She paused. "Well, I'll find out what I can."

"Excellent." Feeling cheered by Vanessa's cooperation, he added, "Thank you for taking on the party at the last minute."

"You're welcome. Did your other caterer cancel again?"

"No. I just needed an elegant touch, and I thought of you."

"Thanks, Daddy," she said, her voice low.

It was the nicest moment they'd shared in a while, and the urge to pull her into his arms and hug her tightly washed over him. Instead, he smiled and brushed his lips across her cheek. "I'll talk to you tomorrow."

"Sure."

When he was in his car and on his way home, he reflected on what he hadn't told Anthony or Vanessa.

The night of the fund-raiser he'd been closely watching that ambulance-chasing leech Broussard. He'd overheard the French phrase *mon ami,* which the scoundrel no doubt thought charming and which the drunken Anthony had no doubt mistakenly translated to *Miami.* He'd also watched Broussard leave the ballroom just moments before his clerk had taken the same path.

At the time, Joseph had thought nothing of the coincidence. But now, in light of Anthony's *dream,* the proximity of the two men shone with a whole new light.

Broussard knew something. He was undoubtedly too crafty to mistake Anthony's dream for the simple ramblings of an impaired man. So…what did he plan to do?

There was only one way to find out.

His MIND ON HIS DATE that evening with Vanessa, Lucas absently picked up his ringing desk phone.

"Mr. Broussard," his secretary said, "Ms. Broussard is on the phone."

That was fast. "Thanks, Kelly."

When he heard the click of the connection, he asked, "You've got news?"

"It wasn't exactly a complicated task," his cousin Jade said.

"For you, I guess not. I got nowhere."

"Did you threaten anybody with a Beretta 9 mm?"

"No."

"There you go."

His cousin, whom he'd only discovered existed after he'd moved to New Orleans to attend Tulane, was an unusual woman in the unusual profession of security expert. She was smart and dangerous, quiet and confident. She had a fierce dedication to those she cared about. Since the group was small, Lucas felt honored to be part of it.

Jade was the one who'd helped him hide part of his past, while letting other parts trickle out. His sort-of-real/sort-of-fictional dark past had garnered a mystique that had served his business well. Which, until recently, was all he'd ever cared about.

Smiling, he leaned back in his chair. "So, what've you got?"

"Three big things. One, Anthony is Anthony Chapman, Douglas's clerk, not an associate at the firm. Two, the widow Switzer and Joseph Douglas, Esquire, are close friends. They dated years ago. There were even rumors of marriage."

Lucas had learned about the widow being a former girlfriend from Vanessa, of course. But the possible marriage was new. "And third?"

"A not-so-pretty scandal that somebody with influence and money doesn't want out."

"There's definitely a connection between Gilbert Switzer and this stripper?"

"Oh, yeah. Candy Anderson is one of the premier dancers at the Flamingo Room, a charming pink-neon gentleman's club off I-95."

"I'll bet you were a big hit there."

"I sent one of my guys. Chicks in clothes make the patrons restless."

"So who'd you threaten with the pistol?"

"The paramedics."

Lucas resisted the urge to comment. Jade did things her

own way for her own reasons. He knew from the past that whenever somebody encouraged restraint, they only netted a glare from those piercing green eyes—a trait that tied them in genetics and temperament.

"I didn't actually shoot anybody," she added into the silence.

"So I don't need to come home and defend you?"

"Where would you find witnesses?"

Nowhere, I'm sure. Jade's security operation handled everything from investigations to bodyguards, and their biggest strength—other than the owner's kick-ass attitude—was discretion.

"So Candy and Gilbert were an item?" he asked, steering the conversation back to the case.

"He used to come into the club a couple of times a month, then once a week, then he'd stay several days. Between lap dances and scotch on the rocks, they took a shine to each other. To some it seemed an obvious big bucks to big boobs attraction. Others claim there was genuine affection."

"So we can figure the truth is somewhere in between."

"Probably. One thing's for certain...the lovely blonde—who dyed her pink locks during her mourning period—with an exceptional pair of double-Ds, is no dummy. She's going to night school to be a paralegal."

"No kidding."

"An interesting development, don't you think?"

"Oh, yeah." If smart, double-D Candy learned about this two-wills business, life was liable to get very interesting for Joseph Douglas.

"Anyway, affair confirmed and confirmed easily. They didn't even seem particularly discreet."

"He was away from his usual circle, his home and family."

"No doubt that played into it. The only thing I really got on top of what you suspected is that she's the one who called 911 in response to Switzer's cardiac arrest in their hotel room."

Lucas's hand tightened around the phone receiver. "She was with him when he died?"

"She was performing CPR when the paramedics arrived."

"Well, well. Paralegal, nurse, stripper."

"She's multitalented all right. The medics shocked him, shot meds into him, everything, but he flatlined. They took him to the hospital, but he was gone long before they got there."

"And the salacious detail missed the newspaper?"

"That's where the old-money-influence thing comes in. All involved were sworn to secrecy for the sake of the family."

"And how did Candy feel about that?"

"She didn't seem to care. She's grief stricken, remember?"

Hearing the cynicism in his cousin's voice, Lucas mirrored it. "Her nipple tassels were droopy."

"I imagine so." She paused, and he could imagine her kicking her gator-skin boots up on her desk. "My guy seemed to think her grief was genuine, though."

"Your guy was distracted by those double-Ds."

"Maybe. But I have no doubt he's seen some pretty good boobs in his time."

"Still, the whole business doesn't paint an upright and proper picture for the Switzer family."

"If Joseph Douglas really has two wills on his hands, he's in just as much trouble."

"It certainly looks that way." He paused, spinning his chair to stare out the window.

"Isn't this what you hoped? What you wanted? You have Douglas's balls to the wall."

"Maybe so." But he couldn't find any joy in it. "I've met the widow. She's elegant and lovely, hurt and confused. She has kids to get through college. She gave up her career at her husband's request, then he couldn't keep his pants zipped, and she's out? As much as I hate it, I think Douglas is doing the right thing."

"But not necessarily the legal thing. And certainly not anything he'd want made public."

"Like I have a right to rat him out."

"It's not about ratting out. It's about leverage." Wearily, she sighed. "Hell, you really are getting a conscience."

"It's about time, don't you think?"

"No."

But Lucas knew she lied. Jade had an unimpeachable moral code. She just wasn't too particular about the means to the end if the cause was justified.

"You have something on him," she said, her voice hard. "Don't let that go."

"I won't. You're coming to visit soon?"

"Sure. When somebody offers me a truckload of money."

"In the meantime, have a beignet for me."

"I will."

"Thanks."

"Let me know how it comes out."

Thinking of Vanessa and how all this would impact her—and them—he simply closed his eyes. "I'll give you an update in a few days. Try not to threaten anybody else."

She snorted. "Yeah. Right."

As Lucas hung up the phone, he was adding up the sequence of events and already calculating his next move.

Gilbert Switzer had had an affair with a stripper in Daytona Beach. Maybe genuine affection had ensued. It hardly mattered legally. The big event was that Switzer got attached. He decided to change his will. He went to his attorney, the esteemed Joseph Douglas, to make that happen. Douglas put him off, or more likely disagreed with him. He obviously didn't want to make those changes, thinking his friend would snap out of the stripper infatuation.

Added to that complication was Douglas's past relationship with Millicent Switzer. Some affection could linger there. His loyalty to his client and friend and his old girlfriend was tested.

Plus, if you knew the man—which Lucas felt he did—Douglas valued tradition and reputation above all else. He must have been appalled at Switzer's request. Leaving out family for some transient affair? That wouldn't be tolerated in Douglas's world.

Of course, he'd cut off his own daughter without a second thought when she hadn't followed the path he wanted her to travel. Though Lucas figured Douglas justified that by assuring himself her desertion would also be transient.

But in the Switzer will business, Douglas had had no control over his client's wishes, so he'd tried to talk him out of it. Maybe he even refused to make the changes. At first.

Switzer was determined, though. He didn't change his mind. He was frustrated by his attorney's stalling. Maybe he threatened to go to another lawyer. So Douglas gave in. He drew up a new will, with his boy Anthony as a witness. But then he never filed the new will as he should have. He swore Anthony to secrecy, knowing his client would come to his senses.

He just didn't count on Gilbert Switzer dying.

Still, Douglas kept his cool. He got the details covered up, even though he couldn't do anything about the nasty affair rumors. He pretended the new will didn't exist and filed the original one with the court.

Yet there were some dangerous loose ends. Even if Douglas destroyed the copies from his office, Lucas couldn't imagine an intelligent man like Switzer not getting a copy of the document. So where was Switzer's copy? There was no way he'd given it to his wife.

What if Anthony blabbed? Which he had. What if Switzer told the stripper about him changing his will? What if the stripper blabbed?

Careless, Douglas. Very careless.

Lucas's secretary buzzed the intercom. "Mr. Broussard, I'm leaving, if that's okay."

"Sure. Thanks, Kelly. Good night."

He sat at his desk for a while longer as the sky beyond his windows turned orange, then pink. He wished he could be out there, on the street, breathing the air, even if it was sticky with humidity. Air-conditioning felt like a luxury. Heat reminded him of his beginnings, of hunger and need, of desperation and anger.

But lives changed. People made decisions every day to ruin or improve their lives, or to just go on with the way things were the day before.

Joseph Douglas had been a good friend, and maybe even a good attorney. He'd just broken the rules in the process.

And damned if Lucas didn't admire him for that.

Shaking off the problem, he packed his briefcase, then headed home to change for his date with Vanessa.

They'd seen each other a lot over the past couple of weeks, and he'd enjoyed every moment. She'd captured his attention, his libido and his emotions. They'd had such vastly different upbringings, yet they had a great deal in common. And while many—especially her family— might consider their relationship forbidden, he recognized her as he never had another.

But she held back. A rebel who feared the unknown. And damned if he knew what to do about it.

When he walked through the back door of the bakery, he promised himself he'd ask her about where their relationship was going. Even though he knew the very thought from a single guy was laughable, and even though he knew he wouldn't.

Her smile or her touch or her body would distract him, and he'd accept what she gave him for the night.

She was standing at the fridge, holding a chocolate cheesecake in one hand and wearing jeans, a T-shirt and an apron—presumably not what she'd be wearing to the nightclub performance they were going to. But then, he could be talked into spending the night in. In his bed. In her bed.

She glanced over her shoulder at him as he crossed the room. Recognition lit her eyes and she smiled broadly.

He slid his hand along the small of her back. *"Bonjour, chère."*

For some reason, the language of his past, the past he'd distanced himself from, he now shared with her.

She slid the cheesecake onto a shelf. "Hi."

He cupped her jaw. "Working late? You're supposed to be taking a bubble bath and dreaming about me." He pressed his lips lightly to hers. "You're supposed to be sliding scented lotion across your body, dabbing perfume between your breasts."

She laid her hands on his chest. "I was thinking I'd do that afterward."

"I like the way you think," he whispered against her lips.

The familiar taste and feel of her slid over him as he deepened the kiss. She curved into him, her breathing quickening, her fingers curling into the fabric of his shirt. Beneath his seeking hands, her body was a delight that never failed to accelerate his pulse.

So much about him was incomplete, even damaged. Why did she continue to let him touch her? Would he ever change his life and himself enough to feel worthy of her? How would he know when he'd been redeemed? And in whose eyes did he want to really shine? His own? The world's?

Gasping, she pulled back. "If we keep this up, we're never going to make it to the club in time for the first set."

He held her tightly against himself. "And that's bad?"

"Even though Mia is the star's cousin, she still had to put forth major bribes to get the tickets. Besides, I promised Peter I'd be there." She kissed him quickly, then spun away. "I just need to change."

Fine by me. Once he got her clothes off, the whole love-making thing always went a lot faster. He started after her.

She held up her hand. "No. You stay here."

"Like I'm the family schnauzer."

"Please, Lucas," she said, backing out of the room. "I promised."

Turning away and saying nothing, he headed toward the storage closet where she kept her liquor. If he was going to be good-humored about lack of sex, *and* be expected to keep his hands to himself on this public outing, he needed a drink.

He wasn't usually this obsessed about sex. Okay, he was a guy and obsessed about sex. But not to this level of neediness and desperation. The deepening intimacy of his and Vanessa's relationship had added a new layer to the pleasure. She was his friend, as well as his lover. They were a couple. The comfort and challenge of that relation-ship had become like breathing to him. Did she feel the same? He wanted to know, but he hesitated to unbalance the peace they'd found together.

He was barely through half a glass of whiskey when she returned. "You want a drink before—" He stared at the vision before him. Blinking, he rolled the cold glass over his now-sweating forehead. *"Bon Dieu."*

She cocked her hip, clad in a sparkly silver miniskirt. "Do what?"

He prayed for strength and promised to call the sisters at St. Francis the next morning and make a generous donation if he managed to recall all the gentlemanly manners they'd tried so hard to teach him. "You're beautiful," he said as he crossed to her and—calling on a deep well of strength—kissed her cheek.

She smells like sex and sin, he noted as he leaned back. Which didn't bode well for the sisters and their rules.

"Are you okay?"

He downed the rest of the whiskey. "Fine."

She was still staring at him oddly. "Maybe I should drive."

"That won't be necessary. I hired a limo."

"You did?"

"Drinking, dancing, late night. I thought it might be a good idea."

She glanced down at herself. "I'm not really dressed for anything that formal."

No, you're dressed for falling into my bed.

Most people would no doubt think her modest black top, silver miniskirt and heeled sandals were just the thing for a nightclub. It was his problem that everything she wore made him automatically picture her in his bed. "You're perfect," he said, somehow maintaining control of his voice.

She smoothed her hands down her skirt. "It's been a while since I've been in a limo."

Having no idea how he was going to survive the night, he set aside his glass, then slid his hand around her waist. "It comes back to you."

10

In the limo, Vanessa sat next to Lucas, her hand on his thigh, her heart thumping with a single glance at his profile.

Not even two weeks. She hadn't even known him two weeks, and yet he'd become central to her life. But as much as she loved every second she spent with him, she was afraid of her feelings growing deeper by the minute.

What was wrong with her? Why couldn't she just enjoy herself?

Mia certainly was. Though she'd spent just as much time with Frankie and David as she had Colin, much to Colin's frustration. He'd e-mailed Vanessa last week and asked what he'd done wrong. Nothing, she'd assured him. Mia just liked playing the field. Her mother was working on her fifth marriage. Maybe it was genetic. Colin had told her he wanted to propose, and Vanessa had assured him that would be a *really* bad idea.

Vanessa thought her roommate should give Colin more of a chance, but maybe variety was the key. The problem was Vanessa didn't want to be with anyone but Lucas.

Tonight he looked sexy as hell in his black pants and a tan shirt, the sleeves rolled back to expose his muscular forearms. *Dangerous and tempting.* That was the way she constantly described him.

She wondered how he'd respond to their night out. Most of their dates involved ordering in or her bringing dinner to his apartment, then they'd make love until dawn. Their world together remained cozy and undisturbed.

Was that why she'd been determined to use her tickets to Peter's show tonight? She definitely wanted to support a friend, but she knew part of her wanted to see how she and Lucas would respond, as a couple, to other people.

Peter was part of the crowd she'd grown up with. His father was a circuit court judge, and he'd been drawn to music rather than law and order. Given his *rebellion,* they'd naturally been drawn to each other, though not in a sexual way. Despite his family's disapproval, Peter had come out of the closet openly in the past few years. He had a partner who supported and loved him, and Vanessa was proud he was following his heart instead of pretending and being ashamed.

Did she have the same courage?

Should she and Lucas decide to come out themselves, her family would never approve of him—even if they knew about his commitment to Brittany Curry and the pro bono work Vanessa had discovered he'd been doing. She wanted so much to repair her relationship with them, and they were making progress. Her mother and father had both hired her to cater in the last two weeks. Her sister had opened up to her about her problems. Was Lucas important enough to sacrifice that progress?

Maybe.

At the moment, though, there was an entirely different

and disturbing element to discuss. Namely, her conversation that afternoon with her father. "My dad's having a party Friday for his cronies," she said.

His gaze met hers. "So I guess you'll be busy that night. I was thinking we could fly down—"

"He's inviting you."

"That's...interesting."

"Isn't it, though? He also asked me about you. He wanted me to ask my friends about you. Essentially, to be a spy for him."

His face was blank of expression as he asked, "What did you say?"

"I said I would." She squeezed his thigh. "I'm not. I just had a weird response to his request."

"You said yes."

"That's what's weird."

"You don't have to agree with him. You don't have to do what he says."

"I know. I don't know what's wrong with me. I guess I should have told him about us."

"It's none of his business."

And it wasn't. But she still felt as though she'd betrayed both Lucas and her father somehow.

"We definitely have a don't-ask-don't-tell policy about my personal life. But I know he's up to something."

"Maybe he just wants to meet me—professionally speaking."

"I doubt it. He knows who you are." When he flinched, she grabbed his hand. "I didn't mean that in a bad way. Though maybe for him you're—" She stopped herself, wondering how to tell him she thought he was amazing, but her family wouldn't be so enthusiastic. "He thinks you're beneath him, and don't be offended by that because most everyone is. Before the fund-raiser—before I knew who you were—he made some comments about you."

"The ambulance chaser."

Out loud—again—it sounded even worse. "Yes."

"Though my sins may be long and varied, Vanessa, I never did that. I never hung out in hospital waiting rooms. I never paid chiropractors to lie on the stand. I never did cheesy television ads to attract people who were hurt, vengeful and poor." He smiled ironically. "But then I never had to. I got a few big judgments, and the clients rolled in. It's no more noble, just less publicly demeaning."

She didn't like how blasé he sounded, how unconcerned about her father's perception of him. He had no idea of the power and influence of Joseph Douglas. "I don't want you anywhere near my father. He could make things difficult for you if he wanted to."

He laid his hand over hers, then picked it up and kissed her palm, his gaze connected with hers the entire time. "I was thinking we could fly down to Miami and have dinner."

"You're not listening."

"I am."

"My father—"

"Doesn't concern me. I'd much rather kiss you…."

Which he did with head-spinning thoroughness. And by the time they walked into the club a few minutes later, she'd set aside her worries about her father. If any man could handle Joseph Douglas, it was Lucas.

Even on a Wednesday the club was already packed, but

when the bouncer checked her ID and took her tickets, he directed her and Lucas to a reserved table in front. Clearly, Mia's bribe to get the tickets had been a good one.

Once they were seated they ordered drinks—whiskey for Lucas, wine for Vanessa—and she glanced around the club. The small tables scattered in front of the stage were filled, and people stood two to three deep at the bars located on opposite sides of the room. Everything was dark paneled and understated. No thumping base, no neon lights. In fact, the only lighting came from canned spotlights recessed into the ceiling, casting pale light on the burgundy carpeting.

"What kind of music does Peter's band play?" Lucas asked.

"They do standards. Lots of Sinatra and Tony Bennett. It's great."

He leaned close and his warmth enveloped her like a soft blanket. "No rap, techno or pyrotechnics?"

"Afraid not."

He slid his hand up her bare thigh. "I'll do my best to muddle along."

"I like dance music and all, but sometimes it's great to hear—" She stopped as his fingers slid beneath the hem of her skirt. "You're going to be good, aren't you?"

He smiled and his hand moved higher. "No."

Vanessa clamped her legs together. "Mia had to bribe Peter's manager to get these seats."

"So you told me." Lucas accepted their drinks from the waitress, then handed hers over. With one hand wrapped around his glass, his other hand returned to its heart-quickening spot.

"We're awfully close to the stage," she reminded him.

One of his fingers glided beneath the edge of her panties. "Close to the action."

Vanessa squirmed. Jeez, the man could make her purr way too quickly and easily. She wasn't crazy about handing over that kind of control.

His finger brushed her labia, and her stomach clenched.

Then again, going with the moment wasn't such a bad thing.

"Hi, Vanessa."

Vanessa's eyes popped open. Staring up and across the table, she saw Tracy Spillman and Brett Riverside.

They'd dated on and off since high school and still made a striking Barbie and Ken kind of couple. Tracy and Vanessa had once been pretty close, but her feud with her family had basically cost her the friendship. Brett was an associate at her father's firm, so his side on the conservative Douglases versus the Lone Rebel Douglas had been a foregone conclusion.

She remembered she'd once been taught manners and rose to her feet, hugging Tracy and kissing Brett's cheek. "It's great to see you both." *Not really, but what else do you say?* She felt Lucas stand beside her. "This is Lucas Broussard. He's a new attorney in town."

Brett, his gaze as cold as ice, exchanged a brief handshake with him. "I know who he is."

Damn, damn, damn. Not now, Brett. Please don't be an ass now. "Did you meet at the fund-raiser? I thought it went really well, didn't you, Tracy?" With her eyes, she implored her old friend to help.

Either Tracy didn't care or she was too dense to detect

the tension. "Your mother seemed pleased," she said, taking extra care not even to acknowledge Lucas.

"She was. Lots of money raised for the children's hospital, I understand. Well, I'd invite you guys to join us, but I don't see any empty chairs to—"

"We wouldn't stay anyway," Brett said.

Then go the hell away, Vanessa wanted to say. What had they come over for anyway? Thankfully, her upper-class arrogance came to the rescue. As she lifted her chin, she linked her arm with Lucas's. "Then isn't it convenient I didn't extend the invitation?"

Lucas, she noted, still hadn't said a word, but as Brett started to turn away, he asked, "Is Douglas that afraid of me, Riverside?"

"You wish."

Vanessa had to clamp her teeth together to keep her jaw from dropping. It was like a fight at fourth-grade recess.

"I'm not suing any of your clients," Lucas said. "At least not at the moment."

Brett puffed his chest out. "We're not afraid of you."

Lucas's eyes gleamed. "Maybe you should be."

Brett held that fierce gaze for a moment or two, then spun away. He grabbed Tracy by the hand and stalked away.

Vanessa trembled with anger and embarrassment. "I'm so sorry. I don't know why they even came over to talk to us."

Lucas put his arms around her waist, pulling her close as he looked down into her face. "To hurt me."

She laid her hands on his chest, surprised to find his heartbeat was slow and steady, not racing like hers. "We used to be friends. What's *with* people?"

"Exactly what I told him. They're afraid."

"While I can imagine you as a scary guy, that's still no excuse to attack somebody."

"They obviously think I deserved it."

She searched his gaze carefully. "But *you* don't think that, do you?"

He held up his hands. "I'm not bleeding. I'll live." He sat, pulling her into her chair next to him. "Forget them."

"You don't deserve to be attacked."

"Maybe. But at one time—"

"Damn it, Lucas, stop." She wrapped her hand around his wrist. "You're the kindest, strongest, most noble man I've ever known."

"Considering you used to hang around jerks like Brett Riverside, I'm not sure that's a compliment."

She glared at him. "You're making light of this."

He cupped her cheek. "My own vigilante." He pressed his lips to hers. "Your faith in me is, quite simply, amazing."

Looking into his deep green eyes, she finally saw some of the hurt he'd been holding back. Her heart flipped over. Crazy emotions surged through her veins, feelings she suppressed. Though, she still wanted to knee Brett in the balls. If he still had any, that is.

Lucas ran his tongue across her bottom lip. His hand slid under her skirt. "Speaking of amazing..."

"We're having a tender moment here."

"I'll be tender."

Thankfully for her sanity, and much to the frustration of her libido, the announcer chose that moment to introduce the band. Lucas was forced to move his hand so he could clap. Vanessa was so thrilled to see Peter decked out in a tailored, pin-striped suit and cool hat, she laughed aloud. The five members of the band were equally entertaining. They even had one guy who held an old-fashioned glass and cigarette while he sang, à la Dean Martin.

In the middle of "Luck Be a Lady," she realized a major consequence of the confrontation with Brett. "My father's going to know about us now," she said in Lucas's ear, when the band took a break. She was trying to remain calm instead of giving in to panic.

"Is that a problem?" he asked, his brows raised.

Yes! "No, I just—" *There goes the temporary truce.* But then it probably wouldn't have lasted anyway. "You definitely shouldn't go to that party Friday night."

"I'm not running from him, Vanessa."

"He'll be mean."

"Not to brag, *chère,* but I can be mean myself."

"You're deliberately going somewhere you know you'll be insulted. Is this some kind of masochistic thing because you aren't proud of your past?"

"I need to find out what he wants."

"So you agree he's up to something and not just curious to meet you."

"I do."

"But earlier you said—"

"Leave your father to me."

Her eyes narrowed as she sipped her wine. "Go along and cook something, dear. Leave the conflicts to the big, strong men."

He drank the rest of his whiskey. "That's not what I meant. This conflict is a professional thing between the two of us."

"A conflict I'm in the middle of."

"I won't put you there," he said coolly, as if insinuating her father wouldn't hesitate. Which he probably wouldn't if it gave him an advantage. "The sooner I face him and let him know I won't be intimidated, the sooner it will pass."

Watching him, the way the teasing lover retreated and the forceful lawyer appeared, another aspect of their encounter with Brett occurred to her. "How did you know Brett was with my father's firm?"

"I told you I researched him."

"You memorized the names of all twenty associates?"

"I believe there are twenty-two, and, no, I didn't. His trying-to-be-fierce Ken-doll face was memorable, though."

Despite her and Lucas's identical assessment of Brett, Vanessa's stomach cramped. She didn't like the way this party standoff was shaping up. She didn't like the suspicion that she'd have to choose between her father and her lover. And despite her fierce defense of him earlier, a small nibble of doubt wormed its way inside. Did Lucas have some secret grudge against her father? Or was it the other way around? Was it possible one or the other was using her as a strategic move on the battlefield?

Could she really fall head over heels for a man who intended to use her? Would she let that happen?

No and no. If Lucas had lied, if he was playing her, she'd know.

But why couldn't she give herself fully to him? Were childhood's fears of rejection and a longing for acceptance still that strong?

"Not even a laugh for the Ken-doll thing?" Lucas asked.

Smiling, she toasted him with her glass. "We're in agreement there."

"But not about your father?"

"I don't like the way he's confronting you. He'll be surrounded by his supporters. You'll be alone."

"You and Mia will be there."

She shook her head. "Just me." And how she needed her partner on this one. "We'd already committed to another party that night, so I'm going solo."

"I'm sorry this will be awkward for you."

"It's not your fault."

"But it would help if I didn't go to the party."

"Maybe, but—"

"I won't go if it's going to hurt you."

Startled, she stared at him. Kind, strong and noble. She wasn't wrong about him. Of all the fake, arrogant, brownnosing people she'd been around most of her life, he was the purest. And wouldn't he laugh at that? "No, you're right. You have to face him sometime. You don't want that hanging over you. Or us."

"Isn't this cozy?"

Vanessa smiled at the sound of her friend's voice and jumped up to hug him. "Peter, you guys are terrific!"

"Thanks, doll. It's a blast."

"Peter, Lucas. Lucas, Peter."

As the two men shook hands, Vanessa noticed the sparkle of appreciation in Peter's eyes. "You always did have premier taste in men," he said.

"And friends," Lucas added.

With Peter beaming, they invited him to join them,

which he agreed he could do for a couple of minutes before
the next set began. After catching up on mutual friends—
and enemies—Peter commented, "I saw Brett and Tracy
stop by."

Vanessa's face flushed with anger and embarrassment. "Yeah."

"You don't have to tell me about them, doll," Peter said,
waving his hand in dismissal. Then, he leaned forward.
"But I wish you would."

Laughing, Vanessa exchanged a glance with Lucas, as
she told her friend about their less-than-pleasant encounter.

"If you're going to have a controversial relationship,
you're going to have problems."

"Controversial?"

"Everybody's no doubt heard the rumors about Lucas—his mysterious beginnings, his rise to rich and privileged." He crinkled his nose. "All that *new* money. You
know these people, Vanessa. Start thinking like them.
Anybody from the outside, anybody different is automatically suspect. And shunning him professionally isn't
enough. They want a personal angle. Why do you think
Brett Riverside just happened to be here tonight?"

The full extent of the rivalry her father obviously felt
toward Lucas washed over her. "He knows we're friends."

"If he recruited one spy, he'll recruit ten." He smiled
with an understanding few who hadn't walked their path
could appreciate. "You made a stand once. You may be
asked to make another."

And it might not be a showdown at the OK Corral, but
Vanessa bet it would be close.

As Lucas handed his keys to the valet in front of the Douglas mansion two days later, an emotion he hadn't felt in a very long time gripped him.

Fear.

Rolling his shoulders, he dismissed the weakness just as quickly as it had appeared. He would focus on his anger and take control of the situation no matter that he was on enemy turf. He held the cards, after all. The information, the power…and Vanessa.

The idea that she could be caught in the middle of this mess between him and her father enraged him. Joseph Douglas had no idea how remarkable his child was, or what she'd become. In the short time Lucas had known Vanessa, he'd witnessed her bailing out her parents at least twice. This, despite the fact that they'd not only shunned her, but discouraged others from patronizing her bakery and using her catering services.

Sabotage. For her own good, naturally.

The absolute control her father demanded was absurd. Though Lucas had grown up pretty much without parents, he preferred making his life his own to having it directed by someone else. Vanessa had tried to do the same, of course, but her parents were blind—or petty—enough not to care.

If Lucas let his rage slip out of control, Douglas could find himself in a precarious position. Lucas had to constantly remind himself to keep Vanessa's well-being foremost in his mind. But he couldn't seem to forget her father didn't treat her the way he should. He certainly didn't respect her or appreciate her.

But he would.

Turning his attention to the house, Lucas couldn't help

a small, ironic shake of his head. The red brick, three-story, white-columned mansion stood on a slight hill, surrounded by stately oaks and magnolias, an immaculate lawn and rows of azalea bushes and hydrangeas. What the hell he was doing in such a setting, he couldn't imagine. He'd probably never get used to the sensation that he didn't belong.

But then that kept him humble, kept him grounded. Without the memory of stale cheese and hardened bread in a rickety trailer, he might have become Joseph Douglas. And that was unacceptable.

He tried not to dwell on the idea that not only didn't he belong in Vanessa's world, he also didn't belong with her.

An older woman dressed in a black-and-white uniform held open the front door of the house. Her face was respectfully blank; she simply nodded as he passed. Lucas fought to ignore his racing heart and concentrate on his hard-won arrogance.

The two-story foyer featured a magnificent, curved white-carpeted stairway, along with numerous works of art and opulent furnishings. Hallways extended straight ahead, then to the right and the left, leading probably to a maze of more moneyed rooms. The maid extended her hand toward the arched doorway in front of him, which undoubtedly led to the party. Before he could walk through, however, Vanessa appeared in front of him.

"Good evening, Mr. Broussard," she said, then gave him an impish grin.

At least this weird night hadn't robbed her of her sense of humor. "Good evening, Ms....?" He gave her a distracted smile. "I'm afraid I've forgotten your name."

Clearly annoyed, she planted her hands on her hips. "Not *that* professional."

They'd agreed to strict professionalism for the night, which, naturally, only made him want to violate the agreement. He was glad to hear she had the same instincts. He stepped close. "Mmm, now that I've gotten a closer look, it's all coming back to me. I'm getting a picture. Lime-green satin-and-lace camisole, tiny panties…"

She flushed. "That was last night."

He eyed her from head to toe, imagining what she had on beneath the black pants and white chef's jacket she wore. "And tonight?"

"Nothing that exciting. Lucas, please be careful."

"No."

She started to lay her hands on his chest, then pulled back at the last minute and glanced over her shoulder. "Franklin Alderson is here. Brett is here. Plus nearly a dozen or so of his buddies. You're going to be surrounded."

Well aware of his position and choosing not to worry her, Lucas craned his neck to look around. "Some place you've got here."

"It's not mine."

"But you have a bedroom here."

"*Had.*"

He frowned. "Is there still a bed? I had plans for that room later."

"I think it's been redecorated as a guest room, but I'm not going up there."

Somehow, he didn't blame her. "Fine by me. We have a confirmed reservation somewhere else."

"Your place?"

"Come to me when you're finished, no matter what time, though I wish you'd let me help you."

"No." She shook her head, her lips drawn into a firm line. "I'm doing this on my own."

Respecting and understanding that, he used the distraction to scoot around her. "Then I'll see you later." She reached for him again, but he stepped back. "How about a drink, Miss Caterer? I could use a shot of whiskey about now."

When she stuck out her tongue, he grinned, then turned to face the lions.

The room he entered was, as expected, large and lavishly decorated. Rich fabrics of gold, navy and burgundy covered the furniture; antique tables made of dark mahogany were scattered about; crystal gleamed beneath the strategically placed lights; walls were painted an elegant shade of the same navy in the sofa.

But it was the men standing throughout the room in small clusters that drew his attention. Fashionably, they'd pulled out all the conservative stops—perfectly cut navy and gray suits, red power ties, gleaming shoes.

He was glad he'd worn black. He was the villain, after all. No point in not playing to the part.

He watched heads turn as he crossed the room. Murmuring followed. Shuffling ensued. With no outward reaction, ignoring them all, Lucas rubbed his hands together.

Let the games begin.

11

LUCAS WALKED STRAIGHT to the bar on the far side of the room. "Jack Daniel's, please, if you have it. On the rocks."

The bartender, dressed in a black tux, nodded his understanding but not before throwing Lucas a quick grin. From the endless pictures he'd been shown on Wednesday night, Lucas recognized him immediately as Peter's partner, Daniel.

Maybe not so alone after all.

Even though Vanessa wanted her parents' love and respect, she clearly wasn't lying down on her rebellion against their methods. Her worry for him, her defense of him, clearly demonstrated the side she'd taken.

Let them come to me, he thought as he sipped his drink. He could stand by the bar and talk to Daniel all night.

"How's your drink, sir?"

"Excellent. You been a bartender long?"

Daniel dipped his head and lowered his voice. "I'm pretty new, but I was trained in New Orleans, so I'm ready for everything."

"Really." Lucas raised his eyebrows and met Daniel's amused gaze. "My old stomping ground."

"So I hear."

"I don't believe we've met," a man said from behind him. When Lucas turned, the guy stuck out his hand. "I'm Bobby Eckland. This party's in honor of my promotion."

Lucas shook his hand. The guy looked either too excited or too caffeinated by his big move up the corporate ladder. "Lucas Broussard."

Bobby paled. "Oh, wow. I've heard of you."

Douglas was obviously trying to lull him into comfort, if this was the guy he'd sent over. "Foster versus the State of Louisiana or Curry versus United Insurance?"

"Both."

"How nice. I have an affection for both."

"Didn't the Foster case involve that blind nurse who'd excelled to administration, then the state tried to fire her a few years before her pension kicked in?"

"It did." She'd never worked again, but then, she hadn't had to. It had only occurred to Lucas years later to ask her if that mattered.

"That case was a great stride forward for the rights of the disabled."

Was this part of the lulling, or was this genuine curiosity? Regardless, he and Bobby dug into a strategy discussion. He'd held others at bay and himself in reserve so long he'd forgotten how interesting professional debate could be. Surely, this wasn't the scenario Douglas had envisioned.

Proof of that came in the form of the man himself.

"Bob, I see you've found our newest resident," Joseph Douglas said as he approached, a fake smile on his face, a crystal tumbler in his hand.

"Y-yes, sir," Bobby said, the expression on his face

giving away his hero worship. "Lucas and I have been discussing some of his past litigations."

"No kidding." Douglas's eyes widened in surprise. "How did you narrow down that massive field?"

"There are a few notable highlights," Lucas said, holding out his hand. "I'm Lucas Broussard. I don't believe we've met, though I certainly know who you are."

Douglas shook his hand. "I understand you've joined Geegan, Duluth and Patterson."

"We're a good fit."

"Crab puff?"

Lucas continued to hold Douglas's gaze even though he could feel Vanessa quivering beside him. "Love one," he said, finally turning to her, selecting an appetizer, then biting in.

The look on Vanessa's face could best be described as tense, apprehensive. But not scared, and for that alone he was cheered.

The caterer's father went rigid. "Just put the tray on the side table, Vanessa. We'll get to it later."

There was an odd, tense moment where the three of them—well, four, if you counted Bobby—stood in absolute silence.

Gesturing with his crab puff—which was probably rude in every circle but the Cypress Bayou Trailer Park— Lucas addressed the others. "Would you like one, Bobby? They're quite good."

Bobby checked Douglas's reaction before he took one from the tray Vanessa still held aloft. Then they spent a moment of silence while they tested the puffs. Was it a momentous culinary occasion? Were the crab puffs that good?

Or bad? Lucas didn't think so. He'd been to a million lame cocktail parties over the years, and he'd tasted bad crab puffs.

No, he was pretty sure the problem was an onset case of Joseph Douglas-itis. No one dared declare the party a success, the new guy cool or the crab puffs acceptable without his approval.

Finally...*finally*, Douglas nodded. "Very nice, Vanessa."

"Oh, I agree, sir," Bobby said, grabbing another. "Lots of crab, not too much breading. You don't get that quality very often. I mean—"

"Could you get me another scotch?" Douglas asked, just as Vanessa had begun to smile beneath Bobby's compliments.

Vanessa glanced at Daniel the bartender, who had no smile and no comment as he made the drink. Saying nothing, she moved on with her tray, and Lucas swore revenge.

"Mr. Douglas," he said, "could I bother you for a moment to discuss a private matter?"

"Of course." Confidence effused in his face as if he'd waited with bated breath for just this moment. "Bobby, if you'll excuse us?"

"Yes, sir," Bobby said as he slinked off.

"Let's go out by the pool," Douglas said, suddenly magnanimous.

Lucas followed him out, buoyed by the low hand slap Daniel gave him before he strode out the door.

The lagoonlike pool area was lit with candles floating on fake lily pads. If Lucas hadn't known the man, he would have thought the setting was charming. As it was, he found it all smacked of contrived sophistication.

"You and Bobby seemed to hit it off," Douglas said.

"I'm sure my impression of Bobby is not why you invited me."

The facade dropped, along with his genial-host expression. "I don't want you anywhere near my daughter."

Obviously Peter had been right, and Douglas's spy network was swift and accurate. "That's for Vanessa to decide."

"It's my job to protect her."

Amused, walking along the edge of the pool, Lucas turned. "Really? Then why haven't you?"

Douglas's face actually mottled. "I won't have her anywhere near you."

Lucas laughed. "That's it? That's the best you can come up with?"

"Don't mock me, boy. You don't want me as an enemy."

"I have no doubt. But that seems a moot point now."

"She's mine."

"She's her own. And, really, you didn't swirl up this party—and no doubt Bobby's unexpected promotion windfall—to talk about Vanessa. What do you want?"

"What do you know about the Switzer will?"

A bit surprised Douglas had thrown in all his cards at once, Lucas stared at the blue-spotlighted pool. "More than I should."

"*What?*"

"I know about Candy, about her heroic CPR effort. I know about cover-ups and bribes. I know Anthony shouldn't have blabbed. I know there are two wills."

"Dear God."

"He may be your last resort."

"Who are you going to tell? What are you going to say?"

"No one. Nothing."

"You don't expect me to believe that."

"Did you honestly think I, of all people, was going to run to the bar crying foul?"

"I wouldn't put anything past you."

"A sensible plan." But then he was keeping quiet for Vanessa and Mrs. Switzer, not out of any need to punish Douglas. "Especially since there's a catch to my silence."

Douglas crossed his arms over his chest. "What? My business contacts? Introduction to my club?"

Lucas resisted the urge to laugh. "I want you to support your daughter."

Clearly confused, he angled his head. "Support her? You mean financially? For your information, Vanessa cut herself off from her family on her own, and I—"

"She doesn't want your money. She wants your support—of her life, her business, her emotional needs. I want you to tell your friends to hire her catering service. I want your office to order pies and pastries for meetings. I want your foundation to sing praises of her culinary abilities and professionalism. And, most of all, I want you to be nice."

"You're joking."

"I know it's a stretch, but I want it done."

"I can't believe you're dragging Vanessa into this."

"I'm simply asking you for a favor. You knew I'd want something for my silence. This is it."

"It's blackmail."

"It's not an unreasonable request, counselor."

"I don't want you anywhere near my daughter."

"Too bad."

Of course, it wasn't the request so much as the person asking it. Was Douglas's pride really worth his reputation?

"It's blackmail," he repeated, his face flushed bright red.

Lucas shrugged.

"Fine," he said finally, furiously, storming away.

Lucas stood by the pool for several minutes. He briefly wondered if he'd done the right thing. He supposed he could have been magnanimous and told Douglas he'd say nothing and ask for nothing in return.

When Douglas calmed down, he'd realize Lucas had done him a favor. He didn't have to wonder when Lucas would suddenly decide to demand a price for his silence.

If she ever learned what he'd done, Vanessa probably wouldn't appreciate his interference. But then he was only nudging father and daughter together. Maintaining their relationship would be up to them. In the meantime, would Lucas regret this risk to renew her bond with her family? Would Douglas convince his daughter that Lucas wasn't good enough for her?

Dear heaven, he hoped not.

Before he left the party—he doubted he'd be welcome any longer—he stopped by the kitchen where Vanessa was standing at the center island arranging toast points piled with caviar on a silver tray.

"What were you and my father talking about? It looked pretty intense."

"Just business."

"Surely you're not going to tell me this is one of those attorney-client discretion things?"

"As a matter of fact..." He rounded the island and slid one arm around her waist. "I just stopped by to tell you I'm leaving."

"Already?"

"I think your father and I have done enough bonding for one night."

She looped her arms around his neck. "Bonding?"

He kissed her briefly, then backed up, breaking their physical connection. He was too susceptible to those seductive blue eyes. "It's not something I can talk about. You're coming by later?"

"I'll even bring leftovers."

"Just remember I get you for dessert."

FOR THE NEXT FEW WEEKS, Vanessa was surprised to find business booming. Her mother's fund-raiser and her father's cocktail party seemed to have been some kind of parental test, which she must have passed.

She was booked for garden-club luncheons, partnership dinners, birthday and retirement parties, even wedding receptions. Most of the new clients could be traced back either to her parents or Lucas. It was kind of bizarre actually, but she wasn't about to complain. Could the understanding and healing she'd wanted for so long finally be in sight?

Late in the afternoon on a Thursday, she was in the bakery's workroom—where she'd spent a lot of time recently—finishing the preparations for a corporate breakfast meeting the next morning, as well as two lunch meetings.

"Wow, these are terrific."

Vanessa looked up to see her sister, enjoying a blueberry muffin, walk through the swinging door. Always impeccably dressed, her sister's pale yellow suit made Vanessa feel like a slob in her jeans and wrinkled T-shirt. "I got some great blueberries from my supplier yesterday."

Her sister plopped onto the bar stool at one end of the island. "How do you keep from getting huge, making this stuff all day?"

"Kickboxing and portion control. What's up?"

Angelica looked around the room. "What makes you think something's up?"

"You don't come by to chat very often."

Her sister grinned. "That's because I didn't know about these muffins."

"How are things between you and Mother?"

Angelica's eyes went blank just before she dropped her muffin and burst into tears. "I screamed at her and ran out."

Vanessa set aside the knife she'd been using to chop basil and pulled her sister into her arms. "It's all right."

"N-no, it's not. She'll hate me. She'll fire me."

"Do you want to tell me what happened?"

She sniffled. "Same thing that happens every afternoon." She leaned back, dabbing at her eyes with her fingertips. Vanessa handed her a paper towel from the counter, and she continued, "She came in my office and told me how to improve my communication skills. I very calmly stood, then screamed at her to get out."

"Sounds like pretty effective communication to me."

"I doubt she'd agree," Angelica said, though she offered a watery smile.

"You did what you had to do."

"Like you?"

"I recall her doing most of the screaming the day I left."

Angelica laughed. "Over a bra."

"It was a pretty great bra. And in all my older-sister wisdom, I think you should go in to the office tomorrow, wear your best power suit—maybe black or red, definitely not dandelion—and ask Mother for a meeting. Tell her how much her criticism hurts you, how you're doing your best and you think you're handling your job just fine. If she's not happy with your performance, then you're prepared to resign."

Angelica's eyes widened. "Resign?"

Vanessa shrugged. Her sister wasn't much of a rebel, but then there were many sacrifices in gaining self-respect. "That's what *I* would do. Maybe you're not ready to go there. Think about it tonight. You could even write out what you plan to say, then you can make a rational decision."

"You know, your standoff with her didn't work out very well."

"But it did. I wouldn't change a thing. And I haven't felt the need to scream at my boss lately."

"You *are* the boss."

Vanessa smiled. "Exactly."

"I'm not sure I'm ready for this."

"Some part of you obviously is."

"Yeah, the psycho yelling part."

"I think there's a feminist in you dying to get out."

Angelica looked horrified.

Shaking her head, Vanessa crossed to the fridge and pulled out a bottle of chardonnay, which she opened.

When she set a full glass in front of her sister, Angelica said, "It's not even five o'clock."

"I won't tell."

Angelica took a bracing sip. "At lunch today Mother said you've been really busy."

"Yeah. It's a lot of her friends calling, too. You know anything about that?"

"I know she's talked to a bunch of people since the fund-raiser. Everybody was really impressed with you."

"No kidding."

"They loved the chocolate fountain—"

Didn't we all?

"—and the ice sculpture and all the food. They all wanted to know where we've been hiding you, as if you've been trapped in the basement or something. I think they just figured out how great you could make their parties, and they were trying to embarrass Mother into recommending you."

"They can't just like my food, call me and book a party?"

"You know they won't. They won't risk Mother's wrath."

"You did."

Angelica waved her hand. "I just blew up today. It's—"

"No, I mean with my business. You always recommended me."

"After I swore you and my friends to secrecy not to tell Mother."

"It was still something," Vanessa said quietly.

"I also know her caterer didn't cancel at the last minute."

"You— *What?* How do you know that?"

"I heard her fire the other company. Apparently, they quoted her one price, then a few weeks before the party tried to raise the rates."

Certain her knees wouldn't hold her, Vanessa sank onto the stool next to her sister.

Angelica pushed her wineglass over. "Have a sip."

Vanessa did. "So, why did she wait till a week before to call me?"

"Pride, I guess. You know Mother. After all the protesting she'd done about your career, she had to think of an excuse to call. Maybe she even thought you wouldn't do her party unless she was desperate."

Vanessa searched her feelings carefully to make sure she wouldn't have been that petty. No. She would have accepted the olive branch. Hadn't she been trying to hold one out for a while now?

"This explains a lot," Vanessa said. "She and Dad both have been so weird lately."

"Weird how?"

"Nice. Friendly. *Family-like.*"

"Definitely weird."

"I guess she's the one who convinced Dad to hire me for every last doughnut gathering at the firm and invite me to lunch three times over the last two weeks."

"Could be."

Vanessa narrowed her eyes. "And why hadn't you bothered to tell me this before now?"

"I'd forgotten about it until you mentioned the parties." She raised her eyebrows. "I *was* in the middle of my own crisis, you know."

"Aren't you still?"

Angelica got another glass from the cabinet and served more wine. "Sorta, but I'm at least ready to make some decisions."

"Good for you."

Angelica raised her glass. "You're a pretty great sister."

Vanessa joined the toast. "Same to you."

"I thought I might find you here."

Vanessa nearly choked at the familiar voice. Setting down her glass, she glanced at the swinging doors, where Elise Douglas stood.

She glanced at her watch. "It's a bit early for cocktails, isn't it, girls?"

"So in Mother strides," Vanessa said while Lucas watched her bustle around his kitchen. "Taking over as usual. But I think Angelica and I were both so stunned—her because of the yelling and me by finding out she willingly hired me—that we didn't argue."

"And why did she hire you?"

"She was tired of the distance between us. She was also tired of paying people outside the family to do what her own daughter could."

"Good ol' Mom—loving and practical."

Vanessa dropped a handful of pasta into a pot of boiling water. "Yeah. It was pretty great actually. She told me how hurt she'd been that I didn't want to be like her, and I told her how hurt I'd been that she wouldn't let me be who I was."

He pulled out lettuce to start the salad. "I'm happy for you, *chère.*"

"It feels different to be on good terms with her. I've stood outside the family for so long."

"That was their mistake, not yours."

She leaned against the counter next to him while he chopped tomatoes. "I made a choice, too."

"You did what you had to do, and they didn't support you. I'm not handing out any awards."

She slid her hand up his arm. "But you're sweet on me, so you're prejudiced."

He glanced at her, and their gazes locked. Her beauty blew him away at times. "So I am."

She smiled, then turned back to the pasta.

Nights like these—where they cooked dinner together at his apartment—had nearly become routine. Whenever he brought up the topic of them as a couple, though, she made a joke, or changed the subject. He was ready for a commitment and wasn't sure how much longer he could force himself to be patient.

"To top it off, Angelica and Mother had a nice talk about their work together. Apparently, there's been some tension between them for a while. I actually mediated." She angled her head. "Do you think I'm losing my rebelliousness?"

"Your what?"

"My rebelliousness. You know, I'm the rebel of the family, and now I'm the *mediator.*"

She whispered this last word, which made him smile. "I think your rep can handle it. Let's eat."

They assembled the dishes at the dining-room table.

Lucas appreciated and treasured so much about Vanessa, and the food she could easily whip up was right near the top. She'd made a big batch of her spicy spaghetti sauce early last week and brought him frozen, two-person portions for them to heat up for dinner. She ate with him nearly every night, and they slept together at his place or hers *every* night.

How long did she want to float in this limbo?

"I think we should—"

"The one thing that—"

They'd both spoken at the same time and exchanged smiles over the sweet, comfortable moment. "You first," Lucas said, leaning back in his chair.

"The one thing that still seems odd is my dad."

He suppressed even the slightest reaction. "Your dad?"

"Mother swears she didn't have anything to do with him suddenly inviting me to lunch or hiring me for parties."

Lucas knew he should keep careful silence here.

"I've been thinking…" Her gaze turned soft, hopeful. "Maybe he's finally realized that Mother's campaign to change me didn't work. Maybe he wants to get to know me better. To be closer."

"Maybe so." *You're lying. What good is a revolution in your life if you lie to the woman who means everything?* "Your father and I did briefly talk about your business the night of that cocktail party. I suggested he would help your relationship if he hired you more often."

"You two talked about me?" she asked, sounding surprised.

"A bit."

She said nothing, sipping her wine. Then she set her

glass down and glared at him. The ice in her eyes chilled him to his toes. "What's going on?"

"Going on?"

"Don't repeat my words back to me. I grew up with a lawyer, remember? And you're suddenly looking very much like a lawyer."

Lucas stood, walking around the table and over to the wall of windows. That critical night a few weeks ago was coming back to haunt him. At the time, he'd wondered if his *request* of Joseph Douglas was a mistake, but in the ensuing weeks he'd seen Vanessa's spirits and confidence rise. She'd repaired the rift she'd longed to close. Douglas had kept his bargain and damned if Lucas didn't believe they'd both benefited.

He'd done a good thing—the *right* thing for once—and still he was positive he was about to hurt Vanessa. The one person he held above all others. The woman he loved.

Maybe he didn't deserve her. Maybe he never would. But he suddenly realized life was a long journey, and he had many more years to prove to her that he was a man worth holding on to. His instincts about helping her and her father repair their relationship had been right and pure. It was his methods that needed work. He prayed that mistake wouldn't cost him the love of his life. After all he'd done, wouldn't it be ironic if a good deed brought him down?

He'd asked himself not long ago whose eyes he wanted to shine in. He knew now. Hers.

Turning, he faced her. He *needed* to face her. "I asked your father to hire you more often, to recommend you to his friends." His gaze connected with hers. "I asked him to be nice to you."

She walked slowly toward him. Her expression was confused, bordering on angry and, yes, hurt. "Nice to me?"

"You told me you wanted to be closer to your family. Every time you talk about them, I see the need, the longing, in your eyes. I wanted to make you happy."

"And my father, after talking to you—his declared enemy—suddenly decided to do as you suggested and be *nice* to me?"

God, why did he know this was going to sound so much worse when he said it than when he'd concocted it? He didn't allow himself the luxury of bracing himself or pausing to gather courage. "No. I asked him to do me a favor, in return for me doing him a favor." He held up his hand as she started to interrupt. "By accident, I learned something about him I shouldn't have. Something that could seriously compromise his professional reputation. I promised silence in return for a favor."

She reached out as if she needed to brace herself against him, then jerked her hand back. "You forced him to do a favor for you?"

He'd given Douglas a choice, hadn't he? No. He really hadn't. "Yes, I did."

Her face paled. Her eyes grew hard, and he was surprised he didn't fall to his knees at her feet. He wasn't shining in her eyes now. Had he just destroyed the one thing that meant everything?

"I hoped if I got you together," he said, "if you spent more time together, you'd repair your relationship."

"Why? Why did you do that?"

"Because it's what you wanted. Because I love you."

12

"YOU *WHAT?*"

"I love you."

Hearing the words again didn't lessen their shock. Why didn't Vanessa feel elation? Shouldn't she be happy? Instead, she was shocked, miserable…manipulated.

And by the only person she'd allowed herself to trust in many years. She was infuriated. Crushed. Overwhelmed. And she was scared.

The feelings she'd fought against were still there, hovering over her heart, threatening to invade forever. Even Lucas's manipulation hadn't killed them. Even though he'd acted just like her parents—he'd rearranged the scenery to suit him, to get what he wanted.

The fact that he justified his actions by saying she benefited infuriated her. It was the same argument she'd heard all her life. *You just listen to me. I know what's best for you….*

"And you love me, too," he said in that same calm, confident tone. "Though I doubt you'll admit it."

One blow followed by more, like the aftershocks of an earthquake. And when had he come to all these fantastic conclusions? Not just this minute. How long had he been holding in his feelings? As long as he'd been keeping the secret about her father? As long as he'd stage-managed and controlled her life and her business?

"Why won't I admit it?" she managed to ask.

"You're scared of loving me. You're afraid I'll reject you. The way your parents did."

Her head snapped back. Her heartbeat raced. "Reject you? Gee, I think you're finally getting the picture." The man was arrogant beyond belief. She tapped her finger against his chest. "I trusted you with my body, my goals and dreams. You took that information and blackmailed my father and manipulated me. Like we're all puppets starring in your exclusive little play. You don't love me. You only want to control me. Like they tried." Her gaze burned into his. "And failed."

"I'm not." He cupped her face. "I was trying to help. I wanted— I *still want* to make you happy."

"Not like this." She stepped back. "Damn it, Lucas, it took me a long time and a lot of courage to get my life where it is. I won't give anybody the chance to mess with that. Not even you."

"I'm not trying to change you. I'm trying to help. And I'd like to point out it worked. You and your father are closer than you have been in years."

She wanted to scream in frustration. The man didn't get it at all. He didn't get *her*. "It's not real! It's based on a lie, on your clever maneuvers. Do you know how it makes me feel that my father hasn't been giving me business and inviting me to lunch because he *wanted* to, but because he was *forced* to?"

"Does it really matter how it started?"

"Yes!" She could feel tears burning at the back of her throat. "He had to be forced into spending time with me."

He shook his head. "He wanted an excuse to see you. He just wasn't happy it was my idea."

"I'm sure." Humiliation still burned in her stomach. "What did you blackmail him with?"

"It wasn't blackmail. It was a favor."

"Yeah, yeah. What do you know?"

He slid his hands into his pockets. "I can't tell you."

Disbelief didn't even begin to cover her reaction. "You're kidding."

"It involves a legal issue—"

"He's not your attorney. You're not obligated to keep silent."

"He's a colleague," he said simply.

She knew now she'd definitely fallen too hard for him, since even through her anger and frustration, her sense of betrayal and confusion, she admired him. "This is what you talked to him about at the cocktail party a couple of weeks ago, isn't it?"

"Yes." He started to close the distance between them, but when she moved away, he stopped. "I'm sorry I hurt you. I just wanted to help."

"You didn't."

He flinched, and she found she didn't want to face his pain. She had plenty of her own. And she couldn't possibly love a man who would go behind her back this way, using the excuse that he only wanted to help.

"I have to go," she said, backing away from him.

"Don't. We need to talk this out."

She snagged her purse off the sofa and headed toward the door. "Too late."

He pursued her into the foyer. "When are you coming back?"

"I'm not." Swallowing, she forced herself to look him in the eye. The confidence was gone from his eyes, replaced by pleading. She opened the door. "I don't trust you anymore. I don't want to see you anymore."

He grabbed her elbow. "Vanessa, please."

The fear she'd felt over his declaration of love washed over her again. Beyond her anger, disappointment and humiliation, she couldn't face his feelings. Or her own. She'd taken on the challenges in her life. Met them. Beat them. She hadn't run away then; she shouldn't run away now.

"Goodbye, Lucas." She pulled out of his grip and closed the door behind her.

You're afraid I'll reject you.

Had she pushed him away so she wouldn't get hurt? If she had, she hadn't done it soon enough. She hurt like hell.

SLUMPING IN HIS CHAIR, Joseph slid aside a stack of files. Work wasn't helping. He wondered if anything would.

Guilt.

The proving of it, avoiding it, the very idea of it, drove his profession. The emotion of it, though, he wasn't generally familiar with.

He'd made the occasional, regrettable decision over the years, but he'd never dwelled on those lapses. He'd used other people's feelings of remorse to win cases, facilitate confessions and even get his way with his family. But there was no escaping the conclusion he'd come to recently.

He'd renewed his relationship with his daughter, and he felt guilty about it.

Worse, he felt the need to confess. He wanted to tell her what had driven him to spend more time with her. And not so he could expose that ruthless blackmailer Lucas Broussard—though that would be a nice side benefit. He wanted to tell her because he didn't want the deception between them. He felt guilty about going forward without telling her the whole story, even if it meant revealing the professionally shaky area of two wills in the Switzer family.

If this feeling was a regular thing, no wonder people were so miserable.

Strong men didn't feel guilt. Strong men led their companies and their families with single-minded confidence. They made the tough, sometimes unpopular decisions and didn't dwell on the past or get caught up in the emotion of the moment.

"Mr. Douglas?" a voice asked from his intercom. "This is Frank at security downstairs. Mrs. Switzer is here to see you."

Great. Another woman he didn't want to face at the moment. Thanks to Vanessa filling up Millie's social calendar and Elise filling up his, he'd avoided her nicely for the past few weeks.

"Mr. Douglas?" the guard asked again.

Joseph sighed. "Send her up."

He thought about fixing himself a drink, but all he needed was for Elise to make another one of her surprise visits and find him sharing scotch with Millie. Instead, he drummed his fingers on his desk and waited for her to appear. To think, by doing the proper thing for a friend, he was suffering instead of being lauded.

The door swung open moments later, and Millie stepped in his office. She wore black slacks and a red silk blouse, and unless his eyesight had gone the way of his ruthlessness, he thought he saw a new flush to her cheeks, a brightness in her eyes.

"I'm sorry to disturb you at work, Joseph," she said once he'd invited her to take the seat opposite his desk. "I called the house, and Elise said you were here."

He suppressed a wince and hoped his wife assumed Millie had called him instead of showing up. He plastered on a polite smile. "I was just about to leave, so your timing is perfect. What can I do for you?"

"I just wanted to thank you for your support over the past few weeks. I blamed myself for Gilbert's affair, you see—at least, at first I did. But knowing that you were taking care of my financial and legal interests, I've been able to focus on myself lately. I've done a lot of thinking and soul searching, which enabled me to let my guilt go."

At least *somebody* had.

"I've rediscovered old friends," she continued, "and I've even gone to parties and nightclubs. Through it all, I've accepted that Gilbert's affair wasn't my fault. I didn't fall short as a wife. It was a decision he made."

How the hell *he'd* helped her realize all that, he had no idea, since he mostly had no idea what she was talking about. Still, he nodded knowingly. "I'm so glad."

"Your daughter is a treasure."

Vanessa. He should have known this turnabout was her doing. She had a knack for making people happy. Had she learned that from him? He frowned, not seeing how, especially since he'd done as much to make her miserable as he had to make her feel good. At least until recently.

If he had to actually thank Broussard for his interference, he'd choke.

"I'd also like to apologize for my, um…behavior when I was here last." Her face reddened. "I was flirting with you, Joseph. Shamelessly. After Gilbert strayed, I didn't think I was desirable anymore. I hope it didn't cause any problems between you and Elise."

"None at all," he lied. He could be magnanimous. Everything had worked out rather well, after all. Millie would get her money. His wife had been more adventurous on Wednesday nights. He'd gotten his daughter back. Vanessa had increased her business. If only he could boot Broussard out of the sunny picture.

Millie rose. "I won't keep you. I just wanted you to know how much I appreciate what you've done."

Joseph stood and captured her hand between both of his. "It was my pleasure."

Pleased with himself and pleased his earlier guilt had faded, he escorted her to the door. As he packed his briefcase, he caught himself humming. When the phone rang, he considered ignoring it, but thought it could be Elise.

"Joseph Douglas," he said into the receiver.

"Mr. Douglas, this is Candy Anderson. We need to talk."

VANESSA WALKED INTO THE BAR, squinting through the smoke for her father. She spotted him sitting on a stool at the far end, slumped over a glass of scotch.

When she'd called him on his cell a few minutes ago, she'd been surprised enough to learn he was at a bar, not at the country club, at home or at the office. But to see *which* bar he'd chosen, she became downright alarmed. It was a serious drinking establishment. No fancy lighting or artful decorations. No leather-covered booths. No low-toned conversations between professionals dressed in tailored suits.

She only got bleary-eyed glances from the few patrons and a glare from the beefy bartender as she moved toward her father.

"Whadya want?" the bartender asked when she'd settled onto a stool.

Figuring a chardonnay would be a lousy bet, she ordered whiskey. She refused to admit she did so because she already missed Lucas. She was furious, not sad. And even if she got past her anger, the situation between her and Lucas would still be impossible.

They'd gotten together for a one-night stand and managed to keep their relationship going for a while longer, but they weren't a long-term couple. Somehow, instead of building intimacy, she'd simply become one of his atonement projects. If he fixed the disowned caterer's estrangement from her family, he'd be a better man.

And no matter how she tried to remember his wonderful qualities, she simply didn't trust him anymore. He'd said nothing the past two weeks as she'd talked about her growing business. He'd said nothing when she'd marveled at how well she and her father were getting along.

You're scared of loving me. You're afraid I'll reject you.

She was pushing him away all right, but she had plenty of better reasons than that one.

The depressing atmosphere definitely called for a little levity. "I hear my boyfriend's been blackmailing you," she said to her father once the bartender moved away.

Her father stared into his half-empty glass. "It hardly matters now."

"But he was."

He shrugged.

The bartender set her whiskey—with no ice—in front of her, and she toasted him before she bravely gulped some down. Gasping, she pounded her chest. "Smooth." He grunted and turned away. "You don't have to worry about him anymore," she said to her father.

He finally looked at her. His eyes were bloodshot, his gaze unfocused. "Why not?"

"We broke up."

"Because of me?"

She shook her head. "We just decided things wouldn't work out."

"I'm sorry."

"So you don't have to be nice anymore."

"I don't need anyone to tell me to be nice to my own daughter," he said stiffly.

"But you did as he asked and steered business my way," she reminded him quietly. "Why? What does he know that's so important to you?"

He glanced down, then back up as he cleared his throat.

"I recommended your business because you're excellent at what you do. And because you deserved better from your mother and me than what you'd been getting." He laid his hand over hers. "Maybe Broussard just reminded me of that."

Vanessa tried to swallow the lump in her throat.

"I never meant to hurt you, Vanessa. I was just stubborn. I wanted you to be part of the foundation, part of the Douglas tradition. And I'm embarrassed that I stood aside and let your mother's arguments with you escalate because I was too damn busy to listen.

"I'm proud that you followed through on your dreams, even though I didn't support you." He gave her a half smile. "You do get your determination from me, you know."

"I figured," she said, dabbing at her eyes as a giant weight lifted off her heart. The things she'd longed to hear for so long were actually being spoken. The rejection she'd felt faded. She was loved and accepted.

"I'm sorry for the past. I've spent the past few weeks trying to make it up to you, though it galls me to admit it took that conniving ambulance chaser to point it out."

"He's not an ambulance chaser, Daddy."

He snorted. "So he says."

So Lucas and her father weren't ever going to be buddy-buddy. But then they weren't likely to run into each other too often now that Lucas was out of her life.

"He'll probably be thrilled it's all going to come out now anyway," he said.

"What's going to come out?"

"A mess." He tossed back the rest of his drink. "See, there are these two wills…"

At the end of his amazing story, Vanessa asked, "So you're meeting the stripper—Candy—Friday?"

"At the house at noon. For obvious reasons, I didn't want her anywhere near the office."

"What do you think she wants?"

"Money, what else? Maybe my career, my reputation." He sighed. "Everything."

Vanessa slid her arm around him. "You won't lose me, Dad. Or Mother. Or Angelica."

He pulled her close. "Thank you," he said gruffly.

Her eyes and chest burned as they held each other. How long had it been since she'd truly hugged her father?

Flaws and mistakes were in the open, and still she and her family loved each other, accepted each other. Her dream had come true. And, damn it, Lucas Broussard had brought it about.

And just why *had* he done it? Was she a project? Was his goal to help or to manipulate? And if the answer was the former, how could she have doubted him? *Why* had she doubted him?

You're afraid I'll reject you.

She wouldn't sabotage herself that way. Would she?

"We'll work this out," she said to her father when she leaned back and dabbed at her eyes. "Even if it's not strictly legal, you tried to do the right thing."

"Not strictly legal? That isn't a comforting statement to an attorney, Vanessa."

"Okay, yeah. So let's think like an attorney." She ignored his exasperated look. "Are you the attorney of record for the whole Switzer family or just Gilbert?"

"All of them. I drew up the damn prenup that even

allowed any of this to happen. I also set up the trusts for the boys, and I prepared and filed Millie's will. I've always provided advice whenever I'm called."

"So, in essence, the duty you were required to perform for Gilbert—changing his will—would have adversely affected your other client, Millie."

"Correct."

"So you chose to protect Millie's interests over Gilbert's."

"But I didn't tell *him* that."

"You tried. He just didn't listen."

"I'm sure the fact that *I tried* will go over well with the Georgia State Bar Association when they decide whether or not to kick me out permanently or just temporarily."

"They wouldn't do that over a little thing like a will."

"A *little* thing? We're talking about nearly thirty million dollars here."

"Wow. No kidding? Jeez, I should have gone to medical school."

"Or married a doctor like your sis—"

"Don't start."

"I've been bossy my whole life. It's hard to give it up in just a few weeks."

To her surprise, he smiled. She returned the smile. Before long, they were both laughing hysterically. "How did our lives get so screwed up in so short a time?" she asked him.

"I have no idea."

"Hey, I'm gonna cut you two off if you don't stop all that," the bartender said, stomping over to scowl at them.

"That's an excellent idea," Vanessa said, standing and feeling only slightly woozy.

Her father tossed a twenty on the bar, then they walked out, arm in arm. Since neither of them were in any shape to drive, they called a cab.

As he held open the door, her father glanced down at her. "I can't believe I'm saying this, but it's possible he wanted to help you more than he wanted to hurt me."

"Who?"

"Lucas Broussard."

Vanessa was beginning to think he might be right, but she needed to figure out what that meant. To her future. To her heart. "You didn't call him an ambulance chaser, Dad."

"Just don't tell anybody I'm going soft."

Vanessa grinned. "I wouldn't dream of it."

ON THURSDAY, two days after the enlightening trip to the bar with her father, Vanessa was running on empty. She whipped up icing for the cinnamon rolls without remembering whether she'd added sugar or salt to the mix.

The peace with her family was better than she'd ever imagined. Last night, she, her parents, her sister and her brother-in-law had shared dinner together. Even though Vanessa could sense her father's slight distraction because of the looming confrontation with Candy Anderson, she doubted anyone else had. They'd had a wonderful time.

After the uplifting interlude, though, she'd returned to brooding about Lucas. She couldn't sleep at night. She couldn't concentrate during the day.

Every time she thought about his manipulation of her, anger jolted through her again. Okay, so maybe he'd expedited her reunion with her family. And maybe he'd done so for unselfish reasons.

But his methods sucked.

So, she worked up her anger as she worked dough in her hands. But when it came time to add cinnamon, icing or—God forbid—chocolate, she remembered how she melted at his smile, how she flickered to life beneath his touch. She remembered the way he'd pampered her, held her, supported her.

Loved her?

Was she throwing away the love of a lifetime because she was—okay maybe she should finally admit it—scared of being rejected?

She'd let her family treat her like crap for years because she didn't want to lose their love. She knew now that her parents had felt just as hurt and betrayed by her leaving home as she'd felt by their lack of support of the nondebutante woman she wanted to be.

And her love life hadn't been so much a victim of her business as it had of her fears. Part of her was sure no man would ever understand her or love her completely. She'd always felt love came with conditions. She had to be this way or that way for people to accept her.

Friends like Mia and Peter had taught her otherwise.

But love doesn't come with guarantees. Lucas might break her heart one day. Was she so afraid of that possibility that she refused even to try?

No doubt that question would keep her up tonight.

Before she could slip from brooding to depressed, though, she heard the back door open, followed by Mia's familiar laughter. She heard the rumble of a male voice, too. Colin? Frank? Mark? She never knew who would come through the door with her partner these days.

She looked up as the workroom door swung open. Colin beamed back at her. Personally, she was rooting for the quiet accountant.

"You look terrible," her roommate announced.

"Gee, Mia, don't gloss it up or anything."

Scowling, Mia walked toward her. "Speaking of gloss, you could use a little on your lips. And your eyes. And those bags under your eyes—"

"So, Colin," Vanessa interrupted with fake brightness, "how are things in the exciting world of accounting?"

"Balanced."

"Balanced?"

"It's an accounting joke. You know, like balancing the books."

She liked the man, but he really needed to come up with some new jokes.

Mia glanced over her shoulder at him. "Would you watch the counter out front for a bit, sweetie? I need to talk to Vanessa."

"Sure." But he gave Mia a lingering kiss before going.

"That poor man is gaga over you."

"Why does that make him poor?"

"Because you're playing with him."

"I am *not*." Her eyes dancing, Mia pressed her lips together as if considering revealing a juicy secret. "He convinced me exclusivity isn't such a bad thing."

"He did, huh? And marriage?"

"Let's not go crazy." She giggled. "But who knows."

"Well, I'll be damned."

"I'm a Renaissance woman. I can grow and change."

"Of course you can." *And maybe you won't be the only*

one. "I think it's terrific. I was rooting for Colin. Even if he does tell lousy jokes."

"He has plenty of other talents, believe me. So, how are things between you and Lucas?"

"There is no me and Lucas, remember?" She'd told Mia everything that had happened, except for the secret Lucas had held over her father. Hopefully, if her father could find a way to talk some sense into Candy Anderson, no one but a select few would ever know.

"Still mad?"

"Yes."

Mia sighed. "I was hoping it would wear off."

"Wear off? The man lied to me, he manipulated me and my father—"

"He knocked some sense into your father, and it was about damn time somebody did." She rolled her eyes upward. "Oh, to be a fly on the wall when Lucas zinged him with what he knew and what he wanted in return."

"He'd probably love a partner for his future blackmail schemes. Why don't you give him a call?"

"If you don't, believe me, I'm going to. He loves you, and you love him, too."

"I'm really getting tired of everyone telling me how I feel."

"You are your father's daughter. Stubborn to the core."

"And don't you forget it."

Sighing, Mia braced her hands on the island and leaned toward her. "Vanessa, what would your father have done to keep this secret quiet?"

It took her a moment to adjust to the change of subject. "Just about anything, I guess."

"He would have introduced Lucas to the Atlanta movers and shakers, the people who've so far shunned him because of his past?"

"Yes."

"He would have gotten him into that silly men's group at the country club?"

"Yes."

"He would have made him a partner in his firm?"

"Probably."

"Yet all Lucas asked him to do was give you business and treat you better."

"But—"

"He asked for something for *you*. Not himself. Not his business. Or the firm he works for." Her eyes somber and determined, she angled her head. "And think about the risk he took in reuniting you with your father, who doesn't like Lucas at all. He risked having you rejoin your family and reject him. He gave you what you wanted most in the world, even though it might mean losing you. If that isn't love, I don't know what is."

"I don't think I like the fact that you've looked at this from an entirely different perspective and made me look petty and difficult at the same time."

Mia smiled weakly. "What are friends for?"

Vanessa leaned heavily against the counter. She remembered Lucas kneeling at her feet and helping her take off her shoes the night of the bachelorette party. Had she fallen in love at that moment? Or had it been the day in his office, when he'd shared his colorful past? Or maybe the first moment she'd seen him, as tempting and gorgeous as chocolate and strawberries.

"I've hurt him badly," she said as the ache in her heart spread.

"No doubt."

"I told him I didn't trust him, and I didn't want to see him anymore."

Mia winced. "Not good."

"He told me he loved me, and I said, *You what?*—like he'd lost his mind or something."

"Oh, brother. Maybe I should write down a few things for you." Mia headed to the utility drawer, presumably for a pen and piece of paper. "We need something poignant. A poem maybe."

"I don't think Lucas—or I—are the *roses are red* type."

Mia tapped a pen against her lips. "No, I suppose not. Maybe an on-your-knees confessional would be more appropriate."

Vanessa winced. "Do I have to actually get on my knees?"

"Stuff your pride, girl. We're talking about your one and only true love here."

"I guess we are." Though she'd probably get kicked out of NOW.

"Ooh, wait." Mia's eyes lit with excitement. "I've got it."

"Does it get me off my knees?"

"You need a gesture of trust. Maybe you could stand with your back to him and fall backward like we used to do at slumber parties."

"Mia, I don't think that—"

Then again…

A gesture of trust. Suddenly, she realized what she needed to do.

Crossing to the phone on the wall, she dialed the familiar number. "Kelly," she said to Lucas's secretary when she answered, "this is Vanessa Douglas. Can you add something to his calendar for tomorrow at lunch?"

NEARLY EMPTY WHISKEY GLASS in hand, Lucas leaned against the balcony wall and stared at the night sky. The drink did nothing to dull the pain. He doubted anything would.

He would see her tomorrow.

Did her call for his help represent hope or doom? Since she'd left an impersonal message with his secretary, he leaned toward the latter.

Yet she'd still called *him,* not one of the dozens of other attorneys her father would no doubt prefer. Was that because he was already in the middle of this will mess?

She'd told him she didn't trust him. Had she changed her mind?

Could he see her and not beg?

He hadn't slept and couldn't remember the last time he'd eaten. He'd fallen apart after she'd left. So many years after escaping poverty, pain and neglect, seeing her turn away had turned him back into that child. His love for her left him vulnerable. Something he promised himself he'd never be again.

He wanted desperately to be angry with her. Instead, he directed his fury inward.

But as he hurled his glass against the balcony floor, he felt some measure of satisfaction seeing the glittering shards littered around his feet.

13

VANESSA PULLED UP to her parents' house at 11:45 the next morning. She was cutting it close, but she didn't want to give her dad too much time to argue about her showing up.

No husband-stealing stripper was going to ruin *her* father's career.

Not to mention take the inheritance that was rightfully Millie's. She and Gilbert had been married more than twenty-five years. No court would award "the other woman" the entire sum of the will. They could challenge the second will, and no doubt win. The problem was that another will suddenly showing up would look major-league suspicious for her father. Besides, nobody wanted this business made public in court.

So, her plan was still the best.

"Vanessa, what are you doing here?" her father said, appearing at the front door before she'd even climbed the porch steps.

She kissed his cheek, then, balancing her trays, scooted around him. "Hi, Dad. I brought lunch."

"Lunch?" he asked incredulously.

"You've heard the expression you catch more flies with honey than vinegar, haven't you?"

"What does that have to do with—"

"You placate more women with chicken-salad croissants than intimidating lawyer talk."

"I'm not serving that woman lunch."

"Of course not. I am." She smiled serenely at his thunderous expression, then sailed into the kitchen. "Did Alice make any tea today?"

"How should I know?" her father answered.

She checked the fridge and found a full crystal pitcher of Alice's famous sweet tea. "Where is Alice today?"

"I sent her to the spa for the afternoon."

Vanessa smiled at the mental picture of stern, serious Alice with a green mud pack on her face and cotton between her toes. "And Mother?"

"She had a garden-club meeting."

"Good. We'll have plenty of privacy for our little meeting."

"It's *my* meeting."

"This woman could affect the entire family, Dad. You should have support. In a close-knit family, each member is there for the other when there's a crisis."

"But I'm in charge, and I don't want—"

She merely raised her eyebrows.

"Thank you for your support," he said, teeth clenched.

"That's better." Smiling, she arranged the croissants on an artful bed of green and red leaf lettuce, then added a scoop of potato salad and a small cup of grapes to the plate. "What do you think?"

"It's—" He stopped, and she watched him physically struggle with his reaction. "It's lovely."

She wondered when he'd notice there were three

plates. She needed to encourage peace now, since he was really going to be annoyed when he found out who else she'd invited. And where was that man, anyway?

"Where does Mother keep the vases?" she asked after she'd searched several cabinets in vain.

"I have no idea."

"You've lived here all your life, Dad."

"You lived here for twenty years, and you don't know where they are," he pointed out. "And what do you need a vase for?"

"The flowers."

"*Flowers?* Vanessa, you absolutely cannot—"

The doorbell interrupted his tirade before it caught significant momentum.

"That's probably her."

"Probably." Though she didn't think so. If she were Candy, she'd arrive ten minutes late just to watch the boys squirm.

Not that she was on Candy's side, but since yesterday she and Mia had turned into something of a detective team, and she'd learned a few things she hoped would give them an advantage in this confrontation.

The chicken salad was just part of the first strike.

"What the hell are *you* doing here?" her father bellowed from the front door.

And the cavalry had just arrived.

She rushed to the foyer before the general imploded. "I invited him," she said quietly, staring past her father to the man she'd laughed, argued and made love with. The man she trusted. And loved.

"Hi, Lucas," she said as their gazes locked.

"I hate to miss a good party," he said, his tone light even though his green eyes were serious, hopeful.

It's going to be all right.

Through all her brooding and planning and worrying over the past three days, part of her had still, somehow, doubted. She'd left him. She'd broken up with him. Why would he help her—and her father—now?

Because he loved her.

Warmth and elation spread through her. Though he hadn't said the words, she felt them through the tender look in his eyes, the one she'd underestimated as simple attraction. The happiness she should have found the first time he'd told her infused her now, reminding her love not only existed in unlikely, even forbidden places, but flourished there.

With her hip, she bumped her stunned father aside and held the door wide. "Come in."

Wearing one of his impeccably tailored charcoal suits, his wavy, black hair framing his handsome face, he walked straight to her. He brushed his lips across her cheek. "You look beautiful, *chère.*"

She grinned. "You're not so bad yourself, counselor." She reached for his hand, shocked to feel a brief tremor. She'd wanted to make a grand gesture, something unexpected and sweet that would prove to Lucas she'd changed and that he'd been an important part of that change. But now she wished she'd talked to him first, given him more reassurance. Trying to let her love shine through her eyes, she gave his hand a supportive squeeze. "Thanks for coming."

"I'm always here for you."

She pressed her lips gently against his. "I think I finally get that."

"I thought you two broke up," her father said with a fierce scowl.

Ignoring him, Vanessa let Lucas's warmth, strength and love infuse her before she turned and led him into the living room. "Why don't we all get comfortable? I expect Candy will be here any moment."

Still holding hands, she and Lucas sat on the sofa. Her father plopped into his favorite chair. "She should be here already. And what's *he* doing here?"

"He's going to be your lawyer."

The stunned look on her father's face was worth every lousy moment she'd been through in her life. "You must be joking."

"Not at all."

"I won't accept—"

"In this case, Dad, *you* are the defendant. If this woman decides to take her case to court, you're going to be in the line of fire. I think it's wise to have your own counsel present for the meeting."

"I can handle this myself."

"Maybe so, but I'd rather you had some help."

"I certainly don't need *his* help."

"He's done pretty good so far. He got our family back together, didn't he? For that, I'll always be grateful." The last of her words she said with a direct look at Lucas. Later, hopefully, she'd be able to tell him how grateful.

Her father leaned forward, bracing his forearms on his thighs. "I can't believe this is happening. I've invited a stripper to lunch in my home. The last man on the planet

I want my daughter involved with is threatening to serve as my lawyer in a suit that hasn't even been filed yet. An ambulance is bound to pull up to the front door any minute, either for me or him and—"

"Dad…" Vanessa began in a warning tone.

"I didn't say ambulance chaser. I'm trying, Vanessa, but you're pushing too far."

The power and drive she'd felt the day of the Red Bra Incident rolled through her. She wasn't worried about how far she'd pushed. Her father would love her, no matter what. Even if he didn't like the way she was snatching his precious control.

The doorbell rang, and both men started to rise.

Relieved this business was finally underway, Vanessa waved her hand. "That's my cue. You ready?"

Even though she hadn't spoken with Lucas directly the day before, the message she'd asked Kelly to give him had explained what she needed.

His gaze on hers, Lucas nodded.

Her father folded his arms over his chest as if he had no intention of participating.

That works for me, Dad, she thought as she headed out of the room. *For once, you need to let somebody else be in charge.*

She took a deep breath as she opened the door, then let it out with a rush of relief when she saw the woman on the other side. She was lovely, not rough or hard looking. Her beautifully cut navy suit highlighted her creamy complexion and white-blond hair. She carried a matching briefcase and wore shining navy pumps.

Having spent time with Millie over the past few weeks,

she knew Gilbert had exceptional taste in women. Apparently, that wasn't a one-shot deal.

And despite the fact that Candy took her clothes off for a living, and NOW most certainly wouldn't approve, Vanessa had the feeling she and this woman would get along quite well.

"Ms. Anderson?" She smiled politely and extended her arm back as she'd seen Alice do a million times. "Please come in."

Without further comment, she led Candy into the living room. Both men stood as they walked in, with Lucas filling in the appropriate introductions.

Vanessa served the luncheon plates at the small oak table near the back of the living room that her parents normally used for bridge parties or summer dinners where everybody could see the pool and cascading fountains without actually having to sweat in the heat and humidity outside.

Though lunch progressed mostly in silence and weather speculation, Candy looked up and smiled as Vanessa picked up her empty plate. "That was delicious. Thank you."

"An old family recipe," Vanessa answered back in polite servant mode.

The moment Vanessa was back in the kitchen, though, she dumped the dirty dishes in the sink and cracked the door so she could see and hear the good stuff.

"Ms. Anderson," Lucas began, all charm and supplication, "my colleague is anxious to get this matter resolved to the satisfaction of all parties. As I'm sure you understand, Mr. Switzer's death has been a terrible shock to his family. We'd rather not unduly burden them with more pain and suffering. Don't you agree?"

Candy delicately pressed her linen napkin to her lips. "I do."

"Excellent. We're prepared to offer you a settlement in the amount of—"

"No, we're not," her father suddenly said, rising from his chair.

Vanessa resisted the urge to bang her head against the kitchen door.

Quickly. That had been her only advice to Lucas, a legal whiz who undoubtedly knew all the moves anyway. *Settle it quickly.* She was sure that if they could be magnanimous, appeal to Candy's sense of guilt as the other woman, then offer her enough money to allow her to finish school and leave the strip club, she'd be satisfied.

"What do you want?" her father went on, full of self-righteous anger. "To cause this family more pain and embarrassment? To steal their inheritance?"

Candy angled her head. "Actually, I'm really curious, Mr. Douglas, why you haven't contacted me before now. I am the rightful heir of Gilbert Switzer's estate, after all."

"You are not. Millicent is."

"But Gilbert changed his will, just three weeks before his death." She reached into her briefcase and pulled out a thick pack of papers, which she laid on the table between them, like the pink elephant running through the courtroom that the jury wasn't supposed to notice. "I have it all right here. Signed by you, and notarized by your clerk."

Her father didn't even glance at the papers. "You don't deserve that money."

She smiled serenely. "As it happens, Mr. Douglas, I agree with you."

IF LUCAS COULD HAVE GIVEN Vanessa a high five, he would have. And Candy Anderson, too, while he was at it.

Women were so amazing. And no two more so than the ones caught up in this mess idiotic Gilbert Switzer had set in motion.

He loved one without reservation. Now, he respected the other.

"I don't want Gilbert's money," Candy said, as if anyone had misunderstood.

And Douglas looked, if not confused, at least like a man who'd just swallowed a guppy.

"I loved him," she said as she rose with a delicate, prideful roll of her shoulders. "No one will ever really understand that. I didn't know he was married at first, and by the time I found out, I was too far gone. I fell hard for his goofy smile and inclination to explain complicated bypass surgery to anyone within hearing distance.

"He gave me a copy of the will a week before he died. We argued about him giving me his money instead of his wife. He insisted, and I temporarily accepted, thinking I could change his mind later." Her gaze landed on Douglas. "I expect you had the same experience, Mr. Douglas."

"I did." He rose, and the Southern gentleman that had been bred in him for generations suddenly appeared. "Please sit back down, Ms. Anderson," he said, laying his hand on the back of her chair. "I've been a complete ass this afternoon, and I apologize. I know we'd both—" he glanced at Lucas, then toward the kitchen door "—we'd *all* like to hear your story."

Lucas looked at the closed door, not at all surprised to see Vanessa breeze through it seconds later. "Vanessa is Mr. Douglas's daughter. She prepared lunch and made sure we behaved."

Vanessa shook Candy's hand, then both women sat. "I also have a stake in making sure they didn't ogle you too much."

"I think they were more afraid of this—" she tapped the will "—than of me."

"With or without any document, you'd make a powerful witness in court, should you wish to pursue a case."

"Vanessa," her father said in warning, "the woman already said she doesn't want the money."

"Why don't you want it?" Vanessa asked, never shifting her attention from Candy.

Though she tried to smile, tears filled her eyes. "Those last moments of his life will haunt me forever. I certainly don't need a check to remind me."

"You can't blame yourself. You tried to save him."

If Lucas hadn't loved Vanessa already, he would have fallen at that moment. She didn't judge people by their appearance or lifestyle, by their bank account or social status. She didn't care about their past. She took them for who they were in that moment. How they treated others, those she cared about and herself.

When her father—and probably Lucas—would have come at Candy with full, legal, intimidating force, Vanessa had recognized a softer path might work better. While it troubled him that he and her father were equals in the ruth-less-tactics department, he also knew their connection with Vanessa would always remind them to question that instinct.

She made Lucas better than before. She strengthened him and challenged him. And reminded him of the rewards of protecting your own, while still serving others. The man he wanted to be, he could be.

If only he had her by his side.

"I just gave him CPR," Candy said, accepting the linen napkin Douglas offered her with a watery smile. "It didn't help."

"You did what you could," Vanessa said gently. "Sometimes that's all there is."

Lucas wondered if Vanessa purposely knew she was comforting him as much as she was Candy.

He'd done what he'd had to do to escape the poverty and neglect he'd sprung from. Sometimes he hadn't made the best choices—just as Candy undoubtedly felt she hadn't by having an affair with a married man—but he'd helped. He'd fought. He'd negotiated when necessary.

He'd worked for his clients as hard as he'd worked for himself. And if he could now share some of that profit and experience with those who couldn't fight for themselves, or didn't know how, then he'd learned something. He'd bettered himself.

He'd earned the right for a slice of happiness of his own.

As they escorted Candy to the door, Vanessa got her e-mail address, promising to send the chicken-salad recipe, and Lucas had no doubt they'd be fast friends in no time. Vanessa had a way of collecting people, causes and friends and whipping them into a supportive network as expertly as she swirled meringue and icing.

Without saying anything, he also added Candy to his projects. There had to be a way to pass money to a few people in Daytona, who'd pass it on to her—enough, at least, for her to finish school without stripping, if she chose to.

But, hell, maybe she felt empowered taking off her clothes. Maybe she wanted to be a proper paralegal by day and a wild woman by night. Whatever her choice, he'd see she found what she needed. Vanessa would no doubt support him.

But would she love him?

Did she love him? She'd kissed him. Her eyes had been soft with welcome. But did she just want to go on as before? He wanted more. He wanted all of her.

He wanted her love. And especially her trust.

"Why did you bring *him* into this?" her father asked the moment the door closed behind Candy.

Vanessa glanced at him for a brief second, then she shrugged. "He was already in. And I knew he'd be polite and respectful to Candy, while you might let your temper rule."

The swallowed-a-guppy look appeared briefly, then he smiled. "And you were right."

She kissed her father's cheek. "And don't you forget it. Now, who's helping with the dishes?"

The spell she'd cast over both him and Joseph—God, it might kill him to refer to him by his first name, but he was doing it anyway—worked its weird magic, since Lucas found himself rinsing dishes and wiping countertops beside a Southern legal icon second only to John Grisham.

He wanted to get Vanessa alone, but this meeting was under her direction, and he wanted her to have control. He'd also like to know how she'd managed everything so smoothly.

"You didn't seem all that surprised by Candy's generosity," he said as he returned the last dish to the cabinets.

A mug of herbal tea cupped between her palms, Vanessa leaned against the counter. "I wasn't—at least not completely."

Joseph slung a towel over his shoulder, then lifted his eyebrows in the same surprised expression Lucas had seen so often in his daughter over the last few weeks.

"I found out she's studying to be a paralegal," Vanessa continued, "so she knows something about the law. If she had a copy of the will, and she intended to challenge Dad in court, why didn't she just file a suit? Why warn the opposing side with a private meeting at his home? She'd had to have retained a lawyer to make the challenge, and he or she certainly wouldn't have recommended such a meeting. So, I assumed she had something else on her mind. I really wasn't sure what until she showed up at the door."

"What did she say?"

"Nothing really. But she wore a beautifully cut suit, one she'd taken time to match with pristine shoes and a briefcase. If she was in this for the money, she would have shown up in a red leather miniskirt."

"How do you know that?" her father asked.

"It's in the rebellion code."

"That red bra."

"There you go."

Her father looked so horrified, she obviously decided he needed comfort. She set aside her mug, crossed to him and hugged him. "Your buddies know lingerie exists, you know."

Joseph reddened. "Under the right circumstances…"

"You guys are cheering about leather and lace with the best of them," she said with a wink. "At the next men's club meeting I'm going to conduct a survey."

"Vanessa, please…"

She kissed him again, then stepped out of his arms. Her gaze shifted to Lucas, and the emotion she'd obviously been hiding peeked out again, as it had the first moment he'd arrived.

His heart jumped in response.

"I also invited Lucas," she said, moving into him, sliding her palms down his sides, "because I wanted him to know I trusted him. I wanted him to know I trusted him with my most precious commodity. My family. And my heart."

Sweet relief rushed over him, and Lucas folded her next to his body. "You have mine, you know."

She slid one hand up his chest, then wrapped it around his neck. "I know. I'm not scared anymore."

"Good, because I'm terrified."

"I can fix that. I'm going to kiss him, Dad," she added.

"Please allow me the courtesy of leaving the room first."

"You'd better hurry."

With a mischievous smile, her lips connected with Lucas's. He poured his fear, frustration, relief and love into her. She gave back her passion. She shared her warmth and her devotion.

The anger and betrayal he'd seen in her eyes the night she'd left his apartment was a sight he never wanted to witness again. He'd work the rest of his life to be sure that never happened. He'd support her and protect her always.

"I want a commitment," he said as they parted for air.

"Okay."

"I want you to move in with me."

"Okay."

He stared down at her in surprise. "You will? Hell, if it was that easy I would have suffered less torture over the past three days."

"Would that question have come before or after you admitted blackmailing my father?"

"Mmm, well—"

She laid her finger over his lips. "Let's just agree to a moratorium on blackmailing."

"I can't be redeemed overnight, you know."

"True. No blackmailing unless I'm a partner, and I get to shower first in the morning."

"Let's not go crazy."

"How about we shower together?"

"Deal. Let's kiss to seal our first compromise."

They did and so thoroughly it took him a few moments to realize they weren't in his kitchen, but in Vanessa's parents'. Breathing hard, with her pinned by his hardened body against the counter, he asked, "What do you say about taking the rest of the day off and continuing to compromise in bed?"

She grinned. "I say, lead on."

They left with only a hollered "See you later, Dad" in the direction of the living room. Lucas figured he might never be completely welcomed in the Douglas mansion, but he also knew both he and Joseph would make their own concessions to keep Vanessa happy.

At his apartment, he led her to the balcony rather than the bedroom.

"Uh, counselor," Vanessa said, glancing around cautiously, "I'm adventurous, but it *is* two o'clock in the afternoon."

"My last memory of being out here wasn't pleasant. I wanted to make a new one."

As he drew her into his arms high above the city he'd decided to make his new home, the love and acceptance he'd waited a lifetime to see beamed back at him from her eyes. He intended to hold on to that precious emotion. "I love you, *chère*."

She traced her finger across his bottom lip. "I love you."

"I'll never stop."

"Me, either."

He leaned close, so their mouths nearly touched. "You were great today. We make a pretty good team."

"We certainly do."

"You didn't eat lunch. Are you sure you're not hungry?"

"I am, but only for dessert."

"You ate all the chocolate the other day."

"Not that kind of dessert. This kind. Just a taste—for now." And she pulled his head toward her waiting lips.

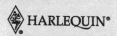

HARLEQUIN® Romance

A family saga begins to unravel
when the doors to the Bella Lucia
Restaurant Empire are opened...

The Brides of Bella Lucia

*A family torn apart by secrets,
reunited by marriage*

AUGUST 2006

Meet Rachel Valentine, in
HAVING THE FRENCHMAN'S BABY
by Rebecca Winters

Find out what happens when a night of passion is followed
by a shocking revelation and an unexpected pregnancy!

SEPTEMBER 2006

The Valentine family saga continues with
THE REBEL PRINCE by Raye Morgan

Page-turning drama…

Exotic, glamorous locations…

Intense emotion and passionate seduction…

Sheikhs, princes and billionaire tycoons…

This summer, may we suggest:

THE SHEIKH'S
DISOBEDIENT BRIDE
by Jane Porter
On sale June.

AT THE GREEK TYCOON'S
BIDDING
by Cathy Williams
On sale July.

THE ITALIAN MILLIONAIRE'S
VIRGIN WIFE
On sale August.

With new titles to choose from every month,
discover a world of romance in our books written
by internationally bestselling authors.

It's the ultimate in quality romance!

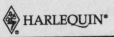

HARLEQUIN®

American ROMANCE®

American Beauties

SORORITY SISTERS,
FRIENDS FOR LIFE

Michele Dunaway

THE MARRIAGE CAMPAIGN

Campaign fund-raiser Lisa Meyer has worked
hard to be her own boss and will let nothing—
especially romance—interfere with her success.
To Mark Smith, Lisa is the perfect candidate for
him to spend his life with. But if she lets herself
fall for Mark, will she lose all she's worked for?
Or will she have a future that's more than
she's ever dreamed of?

On sale August 2006

Also watch for:

THE WEDDING SECRET
On sale December 2006

NINE MONTHS NOTICE
On sale April 2007

Available wherever Harlequin books are sold.

Stability is highly overrated....

Dana Logan's world had always revolved around her children. Now they're all grown up and don't seem to need anything she's able to give them. Struggling to find her new identity, Dana realizes that it's about time for her to get "off her rocker" and begin a new life!

Off Her Rocker

by Jennifer Archer

HN53

Available August 2006
TheNextNovel.com

**Hidden in the secrets of antiquity,
lies the unimagined truth...**

Introducing

ROGUE ANGEL™

a brand-new line filled with mystery
and suspense, action and adventure,
and a fascinating look into history.

And it all begins with DESTINY.

In a sealed crypt in
France, where the
terrifying legend of
the beast of Gevaudan
begins to unravel,
Annja Creed discovers
a stunning artifact
that will seal her destiny.

*Available every other
month starting
July 2006, wherever
you buy books.*

GOLD EAGLE®

GRA1